Rescued by a dog called Flow

Oliver is not happy, he is doing badly at school, his teacher doesn't like him, the other kids tease him and his parents feel worried and disappointed. The only thing that makes life tolerable is Oliver's puppy Flow. The problem with Flow is he has to be kept a secret. Mum and Dad say Oliver has got to do better at school before he can have a pet.

But when a friend is wounded and trapped high up on a hill, both Oliver and Flow display unexpected qualities and nothing is ever quite the same again.

An exciting and moving book.

Other books by Pippa Goodhart

Connor's Eco Home – *Barrington Stoke*
Ratboy – *Barrington Stoke*
The House with No Name – *Barrington Stoke*
Tom Thumb and the Football Team – *Oxford University Press*
Sister Ella – *Oxford University Press*
Snooty Prune – *Oxford University Press*
You Choose (Illustrated by Nick Sharratt) – *Picture Corgi*

PIPPA GOODHART

Rescued by a dog called
FLOW

Illustrated by Anthony Lewis

BARN OWL BOOKS

For Mick, the man and the boy

Originally published by Heinemann in 1994 as *Flow*
This edition published in 2005 by Barn Owl Books
157 Fortis Green Road, London N10 3LX
Barn Owl Books are distributed by Frances Lincoln
4 Torriano Mews, Torriano Avenue, London NW5 2RZ

Text copyright © 1994, 2005 Pippa Goodhart
Illustration copyright © 2005 Anthony Lewis

ISBN 1-903015-47-2

Designed by Douglas Martin
Printed in China for Imago

*Barn Owl Books and Pippa Goodhart
would like to acknowledge the help and support of
Arts Council England in the publishing of this book*

Contents

-1-

I Need a Dog

The day had started hopefully.

"I want a dog," Oliver told his parents at breakfast. "I really want a dog."

"I really want an elephant!" Sally butted in. Then things got silly as they often did between Sally and Dad.

"But you've already got an elephant!" Dad said, pulling Sally's ponytail.

"No, I haven't!"

"Yes, you have. Over there!" Dad said pointing to the old tin trunk by the window where Inkypuss lay in a smug hug of sleep.

"That's Inky, and she's a cat, you twit!" said Sally.

"Oh no, she isn't. I'll prove to you that she's an elephant, shall I?"

Great, thought Oliver. Dad was in a good mood. Perhaps he should ask again about a dog sometime after school. Somehow when Oliver talked with

Dad these days the fun wasn't there. Not as it was for Sally. With Oliver conversations got serious. But perhaps tonight . . .?

"Now to begin with, Sally, what colour are elephants?"

"Grey."

"And what colour is Inkypuss?"

"She's mixed. Black and white mixed."

"And what do you get if you mix black and white?"

"Grey, but . . ."

"Exactly!" said Dad. "There you are then!"

Oliver's gaze wandered through the small panes of the kitchen window to the craggy sunlit fellside beyond. Only a week and a day until school broke up, and then the summer holidays. It would be brilliant if he could have a dog. He only half-listened to Dad and Sally.

"But elephants are big!"

"Ha, but just imagine that you are a mouse, Sally."

"OK, I'm a mouse. So what?"

"So Inkypuss comes around the corner. Is she big, or is she small?"

"Big, but . . ."

"No buts. Told you so. She's an elephant!"

"But she hasn't got a trunk!"

"And what, Sally Clever Clogs Pilkington, is that

thing that she is sleeping on at this very moment?"

"A trunk, but . . ."

"There you are then. Totally proven. We don't need an elephant because we've got one already. Now get ready for school, you two."

I wonder how he'll argue against a dog? thought Oliver. I'll find out this evening.

Then he and Sally had gone to school and everything had gone horribly wrong in a way that was all too familiar.

Oliver sat alone in his classroom. Everyone else was having lunch in the hall, but he was still at his

desk, paper in front of him, pen in his hand, a tight muddle in his head. That muddle was stopping him from writing what he had to write. He couldn't join the others in their lunchtime freedom, not until he'd finished. He could see a ghostly reflection of his face in the window. A stupid face, he thought as he saw the round head topped with scruffy brown hair, round eyes, wide mouth set in a thin unhappy line, and a slightly squashed-looking nose. He'd give anything for a sharp foxy face and red hair like Craig's. Even glasses or a brace on his teeth would make him look more interesting. And then the ghostly picture of Oliver was joined by some ghostly voices. At first Oliver didn't take any particular notice of the mutter of voices that came through the thin wall from the school office next door, but then he heard his name mentioned. He froze still on his chair and listened hard. He recognised the talking voice as his mother's. His fingers were suddenly cold and clammy. Who was she talking to about him? Mum was the school secretary and lots of people came into the office who might talk with her. But he relaxed a bit when he heard the other voice and it wasn't the voice of Mrs Cox, his teacher. It must be Alison Tyson, Craig's mum. She was a school-dinner lady and a friend of his mum's. He could just make out what Mum was saying.

"Mrs Cox does her best, I know, but she's so old-fashioned! She says that Oliver is such a nice boy" and "so helpful when it comes to tidy-up time" but she still insists that he is backward as far as work is concerned. It's such an awful word, isn't it – backward? She thinks that I'm a silly doting mother who won't face the truth when I tell her that I think he's really a very bright lad." Then Mum's voice went quieter and Oliver had to listen hard to hear the next bit.

"But there is certainly something wrong, something holding him back."

Then it was Mrs Tyson's voice.

"Well, Mrs Cox retires next week. Perhaps he'll get a more helpful teacher next time. If he's keen to learn, he might still be able to catch up with the others."

Then it was Mum again.

"Well. I wonder? He used to be so keen in the Infants at his old school, but now he seems to have given up even trying. It's heartbreaking really. There he is at ten years old, struggling to read the books that Sally brings home from school. And she's only five! It's not just his schoolwork either. Only this morning it took him a good half-hour to get his school things together and I'd bet that he's still forgotten half of what he needed!"

Oliver put his fingers in his ears. He'd heard it

all before, sometimes to his face and sometimes in conversations he wasn't meant to hear. But he didn't need to hear it. He knew it for himself. He was "backward", just as Mrs Cox said. He didn't blame her for saying that.

She was right. After all, just as Mum had guessed, here he sat because he had forgotten something. His pencil case. Now he had to write "I will not forget to bring my pencil case to school" five times over. Craig could have done that in two minutes and been back outside playing with the others. But somehow Oliver's brain, his hands, the pen and paper all seemed to make it impossible for him.

His school dinner lay on a tray on the desk beside his work. It was going cold and rubbery. Oliver wasn't hungry anyway. Mrs Cox had said that he was to have the lines correctly and neatly done by the end of lunchtime. If not, she would have to "talk to your parents again about your sloppy attitude and sloppy results, Oliver! After all," she had added, her three chins all wobbling, "it isn't a difficult task for a boy of your age!" But to Oliver it was. So impossibly difficult that he was sweating and felt sick with the effort of trying to write. He looked down at the smeared messy lines that he had written so far, and he didn't know whether or not they were correct. "Could do better," his school reports always said. What Oliver wanted to know was how? How, how, how could he do better?

Suddenly all the other children tumbled out of the hall door to run free in the playground on the other side of the window. Their dancing grey shadows mocked Oliver as they moved across the wall and across him. A big pasty-faced boy came up to the window. He pressed his nose white against the glass and used his fingers to pull his face into an ugly monster shape. His finger spun over his head and he shouted, "Potty Pilkington! Potty Pilkington! His dad's a potter and he's just potty! Pilkington the pillock! Olly the wally!"

Some of the other children in Oliver's class and even some of the younger ones pressed up against the glass too. Oliver felt like the gorilla he had seen in a zoo that banged its head on the wall all day long and the people had all laughed. Now they were laughing at him. And Craig was there too, laughing with the others.

Oliver knew that it was easy to be horrible when you did it as part of a crowd. He had done it to the student teacher last term. His whole class had ganged together and got noisier and naughtier until the teacher had burst into tears. But he hadn't thought Craig would ever do that to him.

Oliver had admired Craig ever since Oliver's

family had moved to the area a year ago. Craig was brave and funny and bright and Oliver wished very much that they could be special friends. He knew that Craig must think him stupid and dull and so he had never yet dared invite him home to play after school. Still, he cherished the hope that it might happen one day. That was why it particularly hurt that Craig was joining the other children in finding Oliver's struggles funny. The jeers went on and on and Oliver clenched his fists.

"Potty Oliver Pilkington! I bet he still uses a potty, too!"

They all laughed again, and Oliver felt his ears burn red. Did they somehow know about the wet sheets in his bed last night? How could they know? In a fury of embarrassment Oliver suddenly picked up the plate of flan, chips and peas and he hurled it at the children at the window. Pudding followed. Then, without waiting to see what sort of a mess he'd made or to see whether they all laughed at that too, he ran.

Oliver ran, slamming doors behind him and not caring who saw him, but he ran fast and far to escape. Beside the school ran a path that went up through a heavy-scented, tall tangle of rhododendron plants. Their big green leaves and huge mauve flowers hid him instantly from the school and the road but he still ran on, slamming through a kissing gate and up on to the open fell. There he stopped at last. He stood still, just panting and letting the warmth of the sun and the breeze of the wind soothe him. He could see the sea from up here. It was several miles away, but on a clear day like today he could look right down the valley towards the flat marshy estuary. The sea beyond was slate grey and out on the horizon was the dark shallow whale-hump of the Isle of Man. Further up the coast the great steaming cooling towers of the nuclear plant poured columns of white cloud into a sky that was otherwise cloudless. It was perfect weather to be up on the fell.

The fell itself was rough ground of steep shale and gentler sloping grassland where sheep grazed, who took no notice at all of Oliver. The path zigzagged up the slope around boulders and bracken towards the mountain-tops, but Oliver liked to leave the path and be really alone. He could explore streams and watch buzzards hovering and swooping on their prey for hours on end and be sure not to meet anybody. Up here he was above and away from the confusions of school and home. Up here he could sort himself out. Sometimes he cried, sometimes he sang, sometimes he went silently and sometimes he talked to himself. Now he surprised himself because out on the fell, walking free, that tight need to cry that had knotted his chest at school eased and his thoughts turned back to his longing for a dog.

I *need* a dog, he thought. A dog to be his companion on these walks over the fells. A dog to play games in the river with. A dog to be at his side and look fierce if anyone came and threatened him. A dog who would love him loyally and uncritically. A dog who would obey his word and never mind what Oliver could or couldn't do at school. He'd asked for a dog before so many times, but now he really ached with the need for one.

Oliver went home at normal going-home time, but his family knew all about his school-dinner throwing and running away. It was not a good moment to ask for a dog. As he stepped through the kitchen door, his mother started.

"Well, Oliver! What have you got to say for yourself this time? Already in trouble and you go and damage school property and then break the law by running away from school! I told Mrs Cox that you would explain and apologise on Monday morning, but I want an explanation from you right now!" She was shouting, and then her face crumpled and her voice went quiet. "Oh, Olly, I just don't know what to do with you any more!"

Sally stood beside Mum, clasping and unclasping her hands in front of her. She hated these Oliver-rows almost as much as Oliver did. Then

Dad came banging in from the garden.

"Where the hell have you been, Oliver?" As he leaned over Oliver and shouted, spit flew out of his mouth and glistened on his beard.

"Your mum came home in tears and I've been searching for you half the afternoon when I should have been working. I'll be up most of the night to catch up now!" Then, when Oliver didn't respond, "Where *were* you? We were worried!"

"I was up on the fell. And please, Dad, Mum, please, *please* can I have a dog?"

His parents laughed bitterly.

"Do you really think," asked his mother, holding Oliver by the shoulders and shaking him slightly, "do you really think that you are responsible enough to look after a dog when you can't even look after yourself?"

Dad just shook his head and pointed firmly towards the stairs.

"Up to your room, Oliver. And the answer to the dog question, once and for all, is a very definite 'No'!"

-2-

I've Come for a Puppy

Oliver chose his puppy the next morning.

Oliver had lain awake most of the night, just thinking. He knew that he could care for a dog and be a good master to it. He also knew that his parents would never allow him to have one. He decided that he would still get one, but it would have to be a secret. He had a vague idea that the dog would eventually be welcomed into the family when he surprised them all with its obedience and the clever things it could do.

Tommy Thompson, one of the farmers up the valley, had some sheepdog puppies to sell. Craig had said that his parents were letting him choose one as his birthday present. Craig's family farmed land near Oliver's home and they had three working sheepdogs already. Craig's puppy was going to be trained to gather sheep and work to the whistle.

Oliver thought that a border collie would suit

his need for a loyal friend. I'll go to Tommy Thompson's in the morning, he decided.

"I'm just going out, Mum!" Oliver shouted over his shoulder as he ran out of the door after breakfast. It was Saturday so he would have to be back in time for his piano lesson at eleven o'clock, but he was going to get the dog sorted first.

He ran through the fields and along by the river, his heart pounding with excitement and his hand clutching the twelve pounds that he had taken from his piggy bank. That had to be enough. It was all he had. He opened the gate to the yard at Tommy's farm and was greeted by woofs coming from one of the old sheds beside the barn. A hole had been worn in the door and a black shiny nose thrust through it and woofed for attention. Behind the door Oliver could hear the yelping and yapping of the puppies.

Oh please, he said inside his head, closing his eyes and biting his lip in a quick urgent prayer, let me have one of them! Then he took a deep breath and knocked at the farmhouse door. Tommy Thompson opened the door.

"Hello, Oliver! Come for eggs for your mum, have you?"

"No. Not today. I've come – well – I've come for a puppy."

"A puppy! Your dad said nothing to me about a puppy when I saw him in the post office yesterday! Still, I'm keen to see them go now. They're a couple of months old and ready to leave their mother. I'm keeping one of them, mind, and young Craig Tyson's due here any minute to choose his, but that still leaves you two to choose from. Come on. I'll let them out for you."

Oliver followed Tommy to the shed door. He knew that he must ask how much the dogs would cost, but he daren't. What if he hadn't enough money?

The shed door opened and out tumbled four tubby snub-nosed little puppies with small whippy tails that spun round their bottoms like helicopter blades. Their mother, Moss, looked very tall and long-nosed, a proper border collie, as she nosed them into order and put up with their thrusting heads butting her tummy in a search for milk. The puppies were all black and white and at first, as Oliver picked up one and then another, he found it hard to tell them apart. But gradually he began to see the differences. One had a comic patch over one eye. I could call him Morgan after the famous pirate, he thought.

"That's the one I'm keeping to train up," said Tommy, so Oliver turned to look at the others. There was one funny little one with no very

distinctive markings, but very distinctive move-
ments. It kept pushing forward and then wriggling
backwards in an odd sort of way. One had a badger-
like stripe down its back. There was a beautiful
one that held its head up high and almost trotted
about like a carriage horse. The patch on its back
looked just like a saddle. I'd call that one Pony,
Oliver thought.

"Are you looking for a bitch or a dog?" asked
Tommy.

"Oh, I don't know. I hadn't thought. Um, a
boy, I think. A dog."

"Right, well then, you've a choice between this

21

one," he said, pointing to Pony, "or this one," and he pointed to the funny one that couldn't make up its mind which way to go. At that moment there was a click of the gate and Moss woofed in welcome as Craig and his dad came into the yard.

"Ah, you've come at just the right time," said Tommy, shaking Mr Tyson by the hand. "Oliver here is just choosing his dog, but I've told him that Craig has the first choice since you spoke to me some time back."

Craig looked surprised to see Oliver with the dogs.

"You never said that you were getting a puppy, Potty! Here, give us a look at them if I'm going to choose mine first."

Craig crouched down beside Oliver. Oliver could see that Craig was just as excited as he was. He watched Craig pick up the warm dumpy wriggling bundles and feel the fast patter of the puppy hearts against his hands and the warm wet tickling of pink tongues.

"They're great, aren't they!" All the wariness had gone from Craig's voice. "Hey, Olly, we could train them together and have competitions! We could even go in for the show! Bet I'd win! My dad knows all about training dogs. I could help you, if you like," he added unexpectedly, and Oliver blushed with pleasure and surprise. But inside he was churning and waiting. Please, please, he thought, don't let him choose Pony! Oliver handed Badger to Craig.

"Look at this one," he said. "Just like a badger!"

"Yea," Craig laughed, "or a skunk!" and he put her down.

"Dog or bitch?" Tommy asked Craig's father.

"I don't mind. Let the boy choose. They both work as well. Would you recommend one more than another, Tommy?"

"Well," said Tommy, "as I've already told Oliver, I'm keeping the one with a patch over his eye for myself. Old Patch – show champion, if you remember – he died last year and I've a fancy for another Patch. Of the others, well, I'd avoid that little funny one. He's the runt and a bit odd, that one. A bit backward, I'd say. Won't make a sheepdog, that's for sure. He never goes in a straight line anywhere!" Craig and his dad laughed. "He'd make a good pet, mind. Just the job for that. But you could never work him. I'd give him away for nothing if anybody'd have him. If not, then I'm afraid he'll have to go in the river. So," he said, "that's down to a choice between these two." He picked up Badger in one hand and Pony in the other.

Oliver saw Craig reach out for Pony, but now he didn't care. His mind was buzzing with what

Tommy had said about the little one. Backward, give him away for nothing, have to go in the river. Oliver's mind was made up.

"I'll have this one, please," he said, and he gently picked up the puppy that they had all laughed at. Craig laughed again

"You really are potty, aren't you! Can't you see it's no good? Go on, have the skunky one. It probably smells like you anyway!"

"That's enough of that, Craig!" warned his dad sternly as he pulled out a cheque-book to pay Tommy. Then he added kindly to Oliver, "If I know anything about animals, Oliver, you'll have got yourself a good loyal friend there."

"I'm calling mine Rex," said Craig. "That means king. What's yours going to be?"

Oliver thought for a moment.

"I don't know yet. I'll have to think."

"Rex. That's a good name for a dog," commented Tommy. "When you choose, Oliver, make it a short name. You need a good short name to call. I've no time for those fancy show names. Trilby Featherstone Dancingpoint the Second, that sort of thing!"

Craig and his dad turned to go, laughing and carrying Pony/Rex away from a rather worried-looking Moss. Tommy turned back to Oliver.

"You keep looking, lad, if you like. You can still

change your mind, you know."

But that wasn't what was making Oliver frown.

"Mr Thompson, can I really have him for free?" Oliver asked.

"Aye, lad. He's yours. I want nothing for that one." Tommy smiled and went to see the Tysons off at the gate.

Oliver held his funny little puppy out to Moss, and they touched big and little noses. Saying goodbye, thought Oliver. He felt a lump in his throat for the puppy, leaving its mother for ever. I'd better go, he thought. He took off his jumper and snugly wrapped the puppy up in its green folds with just his face sticking out at the top and the little whippy tail at the other end. The tail wagged.

"Oh, I'm glad you're happy!" Oliver whispered. "Now it's time to go home."

"Thank you, Mr Thompson," he said as he passed through the gate. "Thank you so much!"

"That's OK, lad. Goodbye now."

A moment later Oliver's hand was suddenly rinsed in warm wet wee. As he walked home he began to think of the problems of looking after the puppy and keeping him a secret from the family. But you're mine now, he thought, and they'll never take you away from me. Never.

−3−

Your Name, Little Puppy, is Flow

Carrying the warm wet bundle home, Oliver thought about names. He walked along with a deep frown on his face and then he stopped by the river where there was a small sliver of beach amongst the pebbles. He carefully put the little puppy down in its jumper wrapping. The puppy dozed snuggly in the sun as Oliver took a stick and slowly and painstakingly wrote something in the

sand. He looked at what he had written and then he carefully wrote something else, glancing now and then at the first bit of writing. At last his face relaxed and smiled.

"That's it!" he said aloud. "Your name, little puppy," he told the sleeping bundle, "is Flow." Oliver rubbed out the writing with a shuffled happy dance while he quietly sang, "Flow, Flow, Flow," then, "Flow, we'd better go!" and he gently picked the puppy up and hurried on his way.

As he entered the field behind the house, Oliver glanced at his watch. Quarter to eleven. Just time to settle Flow in the old back stable and then "arrive home" at the front of the house for his piano lesson. Bother the piano lesson! Still, it was only for half an hour and then he could be back with Flow. The stable door creaked as it opened and Oliver caught his breath for a moment, wondering whether the noise could have been heard in the house. But all stayed still. He breathed easily again and went into the stable. The cobbled floor had some musty old hay on it. The stable was tall, with one cobweb-covered high-up window that let in a streak of sunlight that lit up the top of the room. But down at puppy level it was quite dark. Oliver carefully unwrapped Flow and held him up to talk to him.

"This is your new home, Flow. It won't be for

ever. I'll get you into the house as soon as I can. Promise."

He kissed Flow's warm forehead and laughed as the puppy licked him back. He set Flow down on the hay. He did look tiny down there all alone. Oliver remembered the puppies nudging at Moss for milk. Tommy had said that they were weaned and didn't need their mother's milk any more, but Oliver felt that a drink of milk would comfort the puppy.

"I'll bring you some milk as soon as I can, Flow. Now I've got to go." Glancing at his watch, Oliver knew that he must run.

"See you, my Flow!" and he went out into the bright sunlight, shutting the puppy into the dark cave of a stable behind him. He ran round to the front of the house with his mind hopping and leap-frogging between thoughts.

Hooray, I've got a dog! I've really got a dog!

I do hope he's all right by himself in a strange place.

I'm going to try my hardest ever with the piano, and with everything else, so that Mum and Dad will let me have him properly in the family.

Oliver wondered fleetingly whether his mum would know just by looking at him that he was up to something. His whole body still tingled with the feel of holding Flow, and he felt sure that it must somehow show.

"Come on, Oliver!" called his mother. "Mrs Tumbrill's waiting. Hey, Olly, how did your clean jumper get wet?"

Oliver didn't answer. He ran past her and into the sitting room where he sat down at the piano, and the lesson began.

Oliver's mum hadn't started his piano lessons because Oliver had begged to be allowed to play the piano or anything like that. She had started them because she thought that perhaps he would turn out to be good at music. That would have given him something he could do well, and it might have helped to untangle the knots in his brain that made so many other things hard. It might turn her sulky bad-tempered Oliver back into the enthusiastic happy boy he had once been.

Oliver knew what his mum's plan was, and he wanted it to work. He had started his first few lessons full of hope and had practised hard. But, as with everything else he tried, he was no good at it. When Mrs Tumbrill asked him to sing a tune, he could do it and could do it well. It was the written music, the black dots jumping around the lines on the page, and the two hands doing different things at the same time that threw him completely. However hard he tried, he just couldn't do it, and so piano lessons had turned into the same horrible sort of struggle that school lessons were.

Today, however, Oliver was determined to try really hard. He must please his parents somehow if he was going to be able to keep Flow. But, as usual, the music went badly. Oliver's mind kept turning to Flow and the distant high-pitched yaps that he could hear as he played. Time passed agonisingly slowly, but at last the half-hour was nearly up.

"We'll try that little waltz on page two," said Mrs Tumbrill, sighing as she turned the pages back to the very easy, early part of the music book.

"See if we can at least finish the lesson on a good note," and she laughed at the little joke that she had used and laughed at so many times before. Oliver carefully placed all his fingers on the correct piano keys for the opening bar. He knew this piece off by heart and didn't need to look at the confusing music or think too much about in which direction what hand was going. Thank goodness he'd be able to finish the lesson playing a real tune.

"Dum di di, dum di di," Oliver began, and then "yap yap yap" came from outside the window – an awful lot nearer than the stable. Oliver jumped off the chair and tore out of the room and out of the house.

"Well, really!" exclaimed Mrs Tumbrill, and she went off to the kitchen to have a chat to Mrs Pilkington about her son.

Oliver found Flow peering over the meadow grass and nudging at the gate, just about to come into the garden. His pink mouth was open and piercingly loud yaps were tumbling out of it, one after another. Oliver caught hold of the little puppy and buried the yapping mouth under a hand.

"Shut up, you silly thing! Don't spoil it all!" he whisper-shouted urgently into the puppy's ear. Then, realising that the clasped hand was making Flow even more desperate and the yapping even more fast and furious, he took Flow safely behind a wall and crouched down. He let Flow sit free on his lap and he talked gently to him in a soothing up-and-down tone. The yaps gradually subsided, Oliver chatted on, of plans and of fond nonsense. Flow relaxed and curled down into a compact little bundle in Oliver's lap and suddenly fell asleep.

Oliver sat for some time, ignoring the pins and needles that started to prickle his legs, as he gazed down at Flow. I must remember every mark, every shape of you, he thought. He remembered a sudden moment of panic during the piano lesson when he had tried to conjure up a mental picture of Flow and found that he couldn't do it. He had vividly remembered the feel of the warm solid puppy body and the doggy smell, but he hadn't been able to remember whether the ears were white or black, the paws all the same colour or different. Now he carefully noted every bit of sleeping Flow. He laughed out loud when he noticed how a black patch of fur around Flow's black nose made it look bigger than it really was. I'll draw you some time, he thought, then I'll really remember.

After a while, Oliver gently carried Flow back to the cold dark stable and laid him down, still sleeping soundly, on the hay. He found the old rat-hole that Flow had escaped through and he stuffed it with a stone and some hay. He sneaked into the house for a bowl, a little milk from the fridge and some cold shepherd's pie. I must buy some proper dog food, he thought. And a collar and a lead. And a name tag. How much would his twelve pounds buy? When he got back to the stable, Oliver found Flow wide awake and chasing a big spider across the floor, but he looked up and yapped a welcome to his new master. Nose down and tail up and wagging so fast that it was almost a blur, Flow ate and drank every bit of the food and milk and then licked the bowl so eagerly that it tumbled over on the cobbled floor.

"You have got an appetite!" said Oliver, remembering his granny's remarks about him at tea last Sunday. "Still, I suppose you're a growing boy!"

Then Flow suddenly squatted where he was and did a smelly little poo.

"Oh heck," said Oliver. "I suppose I'll have to get used to this," and he went to fetch a shovel. "Yap yap yap" followed him out of the stable and Oliver gritted his teeth and prayed that they couldn't hear the noise in the house or in Dad's potting barn.

Oliver joined his family for lunch and was told by his half-cross, half-relieved mother that Mrs Tumbrill didn't want to teach him the piano any more.

"I don't think we'll bother finding another teacher, do you?" she asked.

Oliver looked at his mother. Was she cross? But after just a moment of trying to look stern, Mum's face dissolved into a grin.

"You can't pretend that you'll be disappointed to have your Saturday mornings free again, can you, Olly!" Oliver grinned back. "And I'll be saved from having to nag you to practise the piano every day. Oh well," and Mum wiped a pretend tear from under her eye, "I shall just have to resign myself to the fact that my son will never be a musical genius!" She and Oliver laughed together. "I'm sorry for pushing you into it in the first place, love. It was just an idea that I thought might help with the school problems."

"Yes, I know," said Oliver. "I thought it might too, but nothing does." He turned and left the room.

Oliver played with Flow secretly again in the afternoon, and sneaked out in the evening to say goodnight before going to bed.

Next morning Oliver surprised his parents by getting up at seven o'clock, even though it was the weekend.

"He's got some secret," said Sally at breakfast.

"Shut up!" said Oliver.

He rang up Craig, something he had never done before, and was pleased to find Craig wanted to meet.

"Can I come to your place to do some training?" he asked. Sally swung around the post at the bottom of the stairs, chewing her hair and listening to every word.

"With Rex, do you mean?" asked Craig at the other end of the phone. He was puzzled by Oliver not mentioning the dogs.

"Yes. Can I come over?"

"Sure. My mum won't mind. Stay to lunch if you like, and bring your puppy. Has he got a name yet?"

Oliver ignored the name question. He just said, "Great. Yes, please. See you soon, then," and rang off.

"Training for what?" asked Sally.

"For none of your business! But if you must know, it's for the races at the show."

"Oh, that," she said, and she went off, bored if that was all Oliver's secret was.

I'll have to tell them about Flow before the show, Oliver thought, sudden butterflies in his stomach. Still, the show wasn't until the end of the summer holidays and the holidays hadn't even started yet. He'd have to tell them long before that, of course, since the Tyson family and Tommy Thompson knew about Flow. Mum might talk to Mrs Tyson at school again, or Tommy's daughter might say something to Sally. But Oliver pushed those thoughts to the back of his mind and went to tell Dad that he was off to the Tysons' for lunch.

"Fine," said Dad, sitting with a sketch-book on his lap and a pencil in his hand. "There's a competition to design the new range of pottery to be sold at Thornby Hall. It could become a big order and I'm going to have a go at winning it. I'm stuck stupid for ideas, though. All I've tried so far is a pattern of thorns – thorns for Thornby, that sort of idea. Your mother thought of it. It looks pretty, but would you want to put a thorny bramble up to your mouth when you drink from a mug?"

Dad did a little mime of a posh lady with pouted lips, cocking a little finger delicately as she lifted an imaginary cup of tea to her lips, only to shriek in horror as she saw the thorny prickles about to touch her. Oliver laughed.

"I think not," said Dad. "I don't suppose that you've got any brilliant ideas for me, have you,

Olly?" Oliver shook his head. "Sally wanted elephants of course, but I don't think that's quite what they're after! Still, with you out of the way, I just might have a brilliant thought of my own. Off you go then, and don't do anything I wouldn't do!"

If only you knew! thought Oliver.

At Tysons' farm Craig was amused by Oliver's choice of a name for his puppy.

"Flow!" he laughed. "That's a bit of a soppy name for a boy dog! Is it short for Florence?"

"No, it isn't!" said Oliver, but he didn't explain why he had chosen that name.

The puppies were delighted to see each other and began a tumbling, pulling, yapping, play session that left them both so exhausted that they soon curled up together and slept.

"I don't think we'll manage much real training with them yet!" said Craig. "Come on. We'll leave them in the kitchen. Let's get a drink and go outside. My dad says that they're a bit young to teach them much yet anyway, but we can work out how we're going to do it."

They went outside and Oliver sat on the old swing and Craig sat on the grass and pulled out a notebook and pen and they began to plan. They planned to teach the puppies to obey the important commands "sit", "lie down" and "stay" to begin with. Craig also wanted Rex to learn the commands he would need to be a working sheep-dog.

"Ever seen *One Man And His Dog* on telly?" asked Craig. "That's what I want to do. The local show's all right for starters, but national sheepdog competitions are what I really want to go in for, me and Rex."

Oliver thought that just to win the dog and owner's race at the show would be enough to make him happy for life, but he didn't say so.

Seeing Rex in a collar and being fed special tinned puppy food made Oliver realise that he must buy proper food if he was going to look after Flow well. Poor Flow, he thought, as he looked at the tatty bit of rope that he had tied around the puppy's neck. Seeing Craig with his family all playing with Rex made Oliver realise that Flow was missing out in other ways too.

"Don't you spoil the little dog, mind," Mr Tyson kept saying to Craig. "He's to be a working dog, not a pet!" But then he rolled Rex on to his back and rubbed the puppy's tummy just as much as the others. Oliver imagined how Mum, Dad and Sally would love to play like that with Flow, or would they?

Oliver carried a tired Flow home at tea-time, sneaking round the back way and stopping by the wall before passing the back of the house. As he paused to check that nobody was about, an ear-splitting roar rent the sky apart above his head. Oliver recognised the familiar sound of a low-flying jet fighter plane on a practice run. He turned his head to track the jet, already gaining height to rise over the mountains at the top of the valley.

With a yelp of terror Flow found frantic strength and wriggled free from Oliver's grasp. The puppy began to run as fast as his stubby legs would go, straight towards the shelter of the house. Fear suddenly surged through Oliver too. It was a desperate fear that his parents might be just about to find out about Flow in such a way that they would not let him keep the puppy. Oliver ran and grabbed Flow and rushed back to the security of the stable, his heart pounding and his stomach cold. There, guiltily, Oliver turned his mind back to the quivering bundle in his arms and the hard little nose that tried to hide itself by burrowing into the armpit of his jumper. It took some time to settle Flow that evening.

At three o'clock the next morning Oliver awoke in the dark to the sound of thunder. Then lightning streaked zigzag across the sky and dazzled his sleepy eyes. It was followed before he could even begin to count seconds by a roar of thunder that shook the windowpanes. He suddenly remembered little Flow out in the stable.

Oliver jumped out of bed, pulled on a jumper and, hopping across the room as he tugged on his trainers, he pulled back the curtain to reveal dark lashing rain pouring down his window.

Well, there's nothing else for it, he thought, and he opened the window and jumped out. He'd used his window to escape from the house before. The house backed into a hill and so his back bedroom was not far above the field. There was a rather tatty barbed-wire fence in a semicircle behind the window to keep the sheep away from it. Oliver had to scramble through that, ripping something, he didn't stop to see what, on the way. He ran, sodden with the cold rain, through the long grass to the old stable. There, in the dark, lit only occasionally by bright flashes of lightning, he found Flow. He scooped up the trembling terrified puppy and hugged and soothed him for over two hours.

During those cold dark hours he came to a decision. He must tell his parents about Flow. He knew now that he would never be able to keep Flow secret for long. Mum and Dad were bound to find out soon, and the chances of Oliver being allowed to keep Flow would be even worse if they found out by accident rather than from him. He would have to tell them himself, and the sooner the better from Flow's point of view. After all, even in the mere two days since he had got Flow from Tommy

Thompson's, Oliver hadn't really been able to care for him properly. And tomorrow was Monday. He would be at school all day.

"Oh, why can't I do *anything* right?" he sobbed out loud. Then he suddenly felt quite sick as he remembered that Tommy had thought the puppy no good, that he would have to be drowned if nobody would give him a home. If Mum and Dad said no to keeping Flow, then would he find a home with anyone else? Or would he really be killed? Oliver imagined Flow under the water, struggling for breath but drowning as a sackful of stones pinned him down. He tried to shake that dreadful image from his mind. He hugged Flow's small puppy body hard to his chest and, feeling his warmth and heart-beat comfortingly full of life, Oliver told himself that his parents would never let that happen. Oliver returned to his bedroom. He lay staring miserably up at the ceiling with tears pouring down the sides of his face in warm trickles that tickled into his ears and on to his pillow.

"Oh, Flow!" he sobbed, and in those two words expressed a jumble of anger and love and despair and hope that would be resolved one way or the other in the morning.

-4-

Can We Keep Him?

Oliver didn't have to wake the next morning. He'd never gone back to sleep after the thunderstorm. His mind had gone round in circles, thinking about how he could best tell Mum and Dad about Flow. When he heard the alarm go off in their room he jumped straight out of bed and went and knocked on their door.

"Is that you, Olly?" came his mum's sleepy voice. "Come in, love. What is it? Can't you find a clean school shirt?" And then, as Oliver stood silently at the bottom of the bed, she propped herself up to take a bleary look at her son. "Oh, my goodness, Olly! What *have* you been up to? John!" she said, shaking Dad's arm. "John, just look at the state of him!"

Oliver looked down at his wet muddy pyjamas and torn jumper and felt the cracked glaze of dried tears on his cheeks.

"What's happening? What's Olly done,

41

Mummy?" Sally came into the room too. Well, thought Oliver, now everyone is here I'd better get it over with.

"I've got a puppy," he said. "He's lovely and . . ."

"You've got a puppy!" exclaimed his father, suddenly sitting up. He looked comical in spite of his outrage because his hair was all on end. "You say you've *got* a puppy? Since when? Where is it? Where *is* the poor thing, Oliver?"

"I got him on Saturday. From Mr Thompson. Oh, Mum, he's so funny and nice! And . . ." Oliver was almost crying again, even though he had been determined not to. "He's in the stable. I had to look after him in the storm last night. That's why I'm all . . ." Oliver waved his arm up and down his wet tatty clothes. He still had to ask the important question, the only thing that really mattered. He took a deep breath. "Can we keep him, please?" His voice was wobbling slightly.

"Oh yes, please let's!" came Sally's voice, and Oliver knew that he had at least one person on his side.

His father snorted. "If you think . . ."

"Now, John." Mum's voice silenced Dad for a moment. "I think that these children had better go and dress for school while we have a bit of a talk about all this."

So out went Oliver and Sally to dress themselves in nervous silence.

"Oliver!" Dad summoned him to the bedroom door. "Will you go and fetch this dog of yours, please, so that we can at least see what we're talking about."

Oliver couldn't tell from the way that Dad spoke whether or not he would allow Flow to stay. He looked very serious.

"Yes, Dad," he said.

"Can I come too?" asked Sally. The two of them ran through the wet grass to the old stable. It wasn't really big-brother kindliness that made Oliver let Sally be the one to carry Flow into the house. It was the sneaky calculated feeling that his parents might not want to disappoint Sally by giving Flow away, even if they felt that he, Oliver, should be punished for doing exactly what he had been told he must not do. He was quite right. As they went into the kitchen, Mum and Dad looked at the two children and the puppy in silence for a moment. Then Mum's mouth cracked into a smile in spite of herself.

"Oh, John! He is rather sweet!" she said, and she crouched down beside Sally to stroke the puppy's head with one finger.

"What do you call him, Olly?"

"Flow," said Oliver, glancing up at his father. He

knew that he'd won over Mum and Sally, but Dad was a different matter. Dad brushed a hand through his hair and sighed.

"All right, Oliver," he said. "I'll tell you what we'll do in a moment. But I'm far from pleased about this whole thing. You deceived your mum and me. Will I ever be able to trust you again?"

Oliver didn't know what to say. This was awful. He hadn't wanted to deceive his parents. It had simply been the only way he could get a puppy, and

44

his need for a dog had outweighed every other thought.

Dad went on, "You have acted irresponsibly towards us and you have also acted irresponsibly towards the dog. Have you thought about the injections that a puppy should have before it's allowed to meet other dogs and animals?"

Oh no, thought Oliver. All those dogs at the Tysons'!

"Have you considered the cost of caring for him? Or what we will do with him when we go on holiday?" Then, as Oliver remained silent, "Well, *have* you, Oliver?"

Then Dad must have seen Oliver's jaw start to quiver and felt that he had gone far enough. He put a hand on Oliver's shoulder.

"After school, you and I will take Flow to the vet and have him looked at. We'll get advice from him, and then we will make the decision about whether or not to keep him."

"OK," whispered Oliver. "Thanks."

"Can I have a little hold of him, Sally?" asked Dad.

-5-

We'll Show Them!

In spite of everything, Oliver was glad that Flow was out of hiding. Dad had said that he would keep an eye on the puppy while Mum was at work and they had found an old cardboard box and some rags to make him a cosy puppy nest in the kitchen. So as Oliver made his way to school, full of apprehension about what might happen in the day ahead, at least he knew that Flow was being cared for.

It was an odd day at school. Oliver arrived in the classroom just before the buzzer sounded for the start of school. Mrs Cox followed him in. Oliver, who was used to slipping quietly into his seat and staying unnoticed for as long as possible, found that today he was the centre of attention. The other children remembered the dinner-throwing scene and running away, and now they all sat unusually still, watching to see what would happen to Oliver. Some of them had heard from Craig that Oliver had got a puppy, and that added to their curiosity. Oliver looked at Mrs Cox, and a horrible cold dread grabbed at his stomach. Would she tell him off in front of the whole class? Would she set him to write more lines and start that nightmare all over again? But when Mrs Cox spoke, it was in a quiet voice.

"Oliver," she said, "I would like a word with you at break-time. Now, everybody, can we please take the register and collect the dinner money." And the strange silence that had held the class gave way to the more usual hum of activity.

"Good luck!" Craig hissed at Oliver as the break-time buzzer sounded. The other children all ran out to play, leaving Oliver alone with Mrs Cox. Oliver licked his dry lips and waited. But Mrs Cox didn't stand up and shout or wobble her pink chins at him. Instead she invited Oliver to sit down beside her.

"Now," she said, "would you like to try and explain what took place here on Friday?"

So Oliver told her. He told her how he had really tried, but just couldn't do the lines of writing she had asked for. He told her how the other children had laughed at him. He ended by saying that he was sorry. Then he waited to see what Mrs Cox would do. And she surprised him by talking about herself for some time. About how she had taught for very many years and about how it had all got more difficult as new demands were made of teachers, and of how glad she was to be retiring at the end of the week. It was almost as if *she* were trying to apologise to *him* for something, but still Oliver waited for the inevitable punishment. When it came, it wasn't what he had expected.

"Well," said Mrs Cox, "the cleaning-up has been done, and I don't think that it will help either of us if I ask you to write more lines, do you? So, what would you choose to do, Oliver? Some little job just to occupy this break-time?"

Oliver thought. He was about to offer to sharpen all the pencils, then he dared instead to ask, "Could I do a picture, please? Of my new puppy?"

Mrs Cox raised her eyebrows in surprise and then smiled. "Yes," she said, "you can."

Oliver sat alone in the classroom and drew Flow. He drew the big black nose, the dark brown eyes, the silky ears, the fat little body and legs and the little pointy tail. This time he didn't notice whether any of the other children looked in through the window at him or not. He concentrated on drawing, and as he did so he ached deep inside with hope that he could keep Flow and with the fear that he might not be able to.

As he finished the drawing, Oliver glanced up at the clock on the wall. He saw that he still had a couple of minutes before the end of break-time. He took a deep breath, picked-up his writing pencil and carefully wrote "Flow" under his picture. That was the first time he had ever done any writing at school that the teacher hadn't asked for.

At lunchtime Oliver found that Craig wanted to talk to him about puppies. For once it was the other boys who found themselves a bit left out of the conversation. But Oliver was reluctant to talk about Flow too much. He had an uneasy feeling that it would be bad luck to plan ahead when he didn't know whether or not Dad would let him keep him.

Dad brought the car to collect Oliver from school. Flow was on the back seat in his box-bed. Oliver saw that Dad had carefully strapped the safety belt around the box to keep the puppy safe for the journey. Flow tilted his head to one side and looked up at Oliver. His little tail thumped a hello, and Oliver placed a hand on Flow's, warm head and fingered the silky ears and they drove to the vet's.

Dad and Oliver stood beside the table in the vet's surgery as Flow was carefully prodded and examined.

"He seems to be quite healthy. I'll give him the first of the injections in a moment, but I just want to try something first. I'm not sure about this eye," said the vet, and he started shining a light into each of Flow's eyes in turn. Oh no, thought Oliver. his mouth suddenly dry. Don't let there be anything wrong with him!

The vet turned to Oliver. "Have you noticed anything odd in his behaviour at all?"

Oliver paused. Well, there was no use in doing any more lying. He'd done quite enough of that already.

"He does go round in circles a bit, and sometimes backwards," he said.

"To the right or to the left?"

"To the left, I mean the right, well, that way I think," said Oliver, drawing a clockwise circle in the air.

"Yes. That figures. Well, I think you've got yourself a puppy that's blind in the right eye. I can't get any response from it, I'm afraid, and I think that he may be deaf in that ear too. A bit of brain damage at birth, I should think."

Why didn't I guess? wondered Oliver. Of course! Tommy Thompson and Craig had been right when they said that something was wrong with him. Poor little Flow! But what was the vet saying now?

"He'll never make a show dog or a working dog, obviously, but I've seen deaf and blind animals make good pets. Do you still want him, Mr Pilkington? Should I give him the injections?"

Oliver looked beseechingly up at his father. Dad

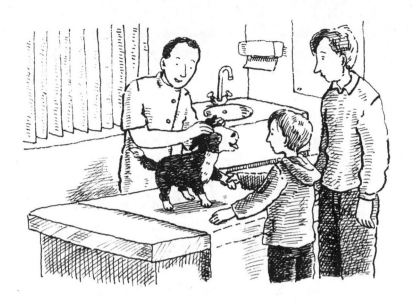

put a hand on Flow's head.

"Yes. We want him, thanks."

"Oh, Dad!" Oliver let out the breath he hadn't realised he had been holding. "Thanks!" He almost wanted to cry all over again!

Back in the car. Dad added a condition.

"You can keep Flow, Olly. but I want something in return. You know how worried we are about your schoolwork? I'm afraid that academic results matter in today's world and you are going to slip behind all your schoolmates if we can't do something about this reading and writing problem of yours. And maths, too. What I suggest is that, in return for having Flow, you promise to try your hardest with me for one hour every day of the

holidays, and we'll see what we can do together."
He saw Oliver frown. "It won't be like schoolwork,
or even homework, I promise. We'll do the work
together, you and I, and I'll try to make it fun.
Think of it as 'Flow-work' if you like. You putting
in some effort in payment for Flow."

Then unexpectedly, Dad added, "You know,
Olly, I do understand what it's like. I had the
same struggle at school myself and I never did well
when it came to exams. That's why I ended up as
a potter. I don't regret that, mind you. I enjoy my
work, as you well know. Potty about it, as your
friends would say. But I'd like you to have more
choice of jobs. So please let's see if I can help you."

"OK, Dad." Oliver didn't like the idea of work
intruding into precious holiday time. But as long
as he had Flow, he felt that he wouldn't mind anything too much. He gently stroked Flow's head as
it rested heavily on his leg. No, he didn't mind.
And whatever the vet had said, Oliver was more
determined than ever that Flow should win something at the show. There was nothing wrong with
Flow's legs for running and, when Oliver looked at
his puppy's steady, trusting, one-eyed gaze, he
knew that he could train Flow to be obedient. They
would make a great team. We'll show them, he
thought. We'll surprise them all!

-6-

Gangly Pair of Boys

The summer holidays began and the days took on a pattern for Oliver that revolved around work and Flow. Dad would take Oliver to the potting barn, and they would sit together and work at his reading and writing. It was always a wrench for Oliver to leave Flow playing with Sally and turn to the books and pens that he had come to dread. But the barn was so different from school. The smell of damp clay, the the stacked shelves of drying pots, the bins of coloured glaze, the potting wheel and work bench lit by sunlight pouring in from the skylight in the roof, made it a special place that Oliver had loved ever since they moved to their new home. And to his surprise Oliver found that his hour each day with Dad could be fun. The work was so different from school too. Dad and Oliver had even made a clay alphabet, shaping each letter and then drying, glazing and firing it. Oliver had painted a glaze picture of Flow on the F.

Sometimes they would eat a sandwich lunch in the barn and play I-spy while they ate.

"One sandwich left," said Dad. "I'll play you for it. If you win the next round you get the sandwich. If I win then I get it."

"OK," agreed Oliver.

Dad grinned. "I spy with my little eye something beginning with Q."

Oliver looked all around. Q? There was absolutely nothing that he could see that began with Q.

"Do you give in?" laughed Dad.

Oliver wanted that last sandwich. "Have you got a quill somewhere?" he guessed a bit desperately.

"No."

"Oh, I give up then. What is it?"

"It's the cucumber in the sandwich!" Oliver frowned and Dad laughed. "Well, cucumber begins with the sound Q, even if you spell it with a C!"

"Oh, Dad!" Oliver punched Dad on the arm and quickly grabbed the last sandwich. "You can't win if you cheat!"

"That's quite true. It's all yours!" agreed Dad.

Oliver enjoyed his time with Dad, but he was always eager to race back to the house and collect Flow for a training session. The training was a serious business because Oliver really did intend to win some of the races at the show. He would lie in bed each night, dreaming of his moment of glory in front of the children and teachers from school as he and Flow pounded through the white tape to win the dog and owner's race. And Flow would "flow" effortlessly over the obstacles of the obstacle race. And they'll all think that's why he's called Flow! Oliver thought, and he smiled to himself.

He imagined the final ceremony of the day when cups and medals would be presented to the best-dressed huntsman, the winning fell runner, and the champion dog – Flow, of course! Oliver would shake the hand of Colonel George and pat Flow on the head with the hand that wasn't holding the fine silver cup. Flow would gaze adoringly up at his master and Oliver would allow himself a small modest smile. And with the applause ringing in his dreaming ears, Oliver would turn over and go happily to sleep. For once in his life Oliver really felt that he could be a winner. Flow was a bright puppy and the eager way that he looked up to Oliver to see what was wanted made Oliver happier than he had felt in a long time.

Up on the open fell, up and down the garden, in the field at Tysons' farm and on a lead into the village, Oliver and Flow worked tirelessly. Dad had warned Oliver that even by the end of August when the show was held Flow would "still be far from fully grown and it wasn't fair to expect him to win against adult dogs. There was the blindness and deafness to be taken into account, too. But Oliver was secretly confident that Flow could and would be a winner in spite of all that. Mum had given him a surprise present to help with the training – a stop watch. Just as his dad managed to make some of his own reading and writing lessons fun, so Oliver turned a lot of Flow's training into games, too. Best of all were the days when Oliver and Flow joined Craig and Rex in a field and "did the show". They took it in turns to hold a fist up to their mouths as a pretend microphone to provide a running commentary.

"And here we have Master Oliver Pilkington of Hermit House, putting his fine young sheepdog, Flow, through his paces. And . . . they're off! It's against the clock, ladies and gentlemen, and they've made a fine start. As they near the first boulder we see Flow gather himself for the jump, and he's up and over with room to spare. Now, can he race through that pipe or will he refuse to leave his master and make a pig's ear of it as he usually does?!"

Craig laughed at this point. His Rex always raced straight through with no hesitation, but Flow would glance at Oliver as if he were saying, "Do you really want me to leave you and go through there on my own?" As often as not he would refuse.

"Go on, Flow!" urged Oliver. "See you at the other end. Go!"

The droning commentary voice began again. "Aaaand he's done it! A miracle! We approach the final hurdle now and – hey – cripes!" It was Craig's real voice again. "Are you all right,Potty? He was going really well too!"

It was a familiar problem. A sudden sound from a disturbed curlew in the grass over to the right had startled Flow into going round in a circle as he brought his good ear and eye round to investigate. Oliver, who had been running on Flow's right side, had been tripped and now sprawled on the ground.

"Flow, you stupid dog!" he shouted at the puppy. Flow cowered apologetically. At moments like this Oliver was aware of a strong urge to hit Flow hard, just to relieve his own feeling of frustration, but he knew it would do more harm than good. Instead he kicked at the ground and shook a fist at Flow.

"What *can* I do, Craig? He's really good at most of it now, until he starts going round in stupid circles!"

"I always told you he was as potty as you! You ask your dad. Pots go round in circles, don't they?"

"Come on, let's try again."

"All right, but it's mmmyy turn now."

"OK, hand over, the microphone," and they were off again with Oliver doing the talking this time.

"Now Mr Craig Tyson enters the ring with the youngest dog from the Tyson kennel. Young Rex prances boldly into the ring and prepares himself for the off. On your marks. Get set. (Oh, hang on a mo, the watch has got stuck. There. Got it. OK.) On your marks, get set, go! And they're off, running fast for the first hurdle. We note from the watch that they are not as fast as the previous competitors," Craig stuck his tongue out at Oliver for that, "but Rex takes the boulder in one leap and heads for the pipe. With no hesitation he races into the pipe, aaaand . . . out the other end where he is reunited with Mr Tyson. And together they run towards the final jump but, oh dear, we have another disaster! Rex has seen a rabbit and he's off over the fell after it with Mr Tyson following!"

It was Oliver's turn to laugh as Craig raced after his dog, shouting as Rex ignored his commands. Flow and Oliver chased after them too. As usual Oliver found that he and Flow could gain on Craig and Rex. They really were the faster pair, thought Oliver smugly. But this was the first time that they had run together and Flow had overtaken Oliver. Both puppies had been getting taller and more leggy. day by day and now Flow's four legs could beat Oliver's two.

By the end of August he'll be really fast, thought Oliver with satisfaction. And if he can run faster than me, then the real race in the dog and owner's race will be me against the other owners. He made up his mind to do some running of his own. It'll be both of us who are tested in that one. He knew that he could run faster than Craig, but even some adults went in for the dog and owner's race, and they might be really fast.

Halfway through the holidays Oliver was feeling fairly happy about the way that Flow's training was going. Both Flow and Rex had learned all the commands but, surprisingly, it was the larger, more confident Rex who was the less reliable of the two. He would obey when he felt like it but he had an independent streak in him that meant Craig could never completely rely on his doing what he was told. Flow, as the naturally less able puppy, hampered by disability and size, actually made up for that by his eagerness to please. That and Oliver's intensive training had made Flow into a dog who would obey commands.

He was no problem with the sheep on the fell either. A fierce butt early on from a mother sheep, who had seen little Flow sniffing at her lamb, had taught him that he must never interfere with sheep. So now Oliver could leave him off the lead and Flow would walk to heel or run free as Oliver commanded. The only big problem that remained was the way that Flow would suddenly go round in a circle when startled by a sound or smell on his right side. Craig doubled up laughing every time it happened. Oliver puzzled long and hard about how he could overcome the problem. In the end he went and asked advice from Craig's dad.

"There's only one way you'll cure that, and that's by ordinary training, just like all the rest of it. Give him practice with different distractions,

keep a close hold on his collar and make him keep walking to heel whatever noises are going on. And if he does it well, reward him. That'll do it. You'll see. It's how they train those police horses not to be startled by sudden noises. It's just a matter of habit. Get my Craig to help you. You'll need one person to control the dog and another to make noises."

That led to a new training pattern. This time Oliver, tight-lipped and concentrating hard, held Flow walking close to heel while Craig did his best to distract the dog. Craig shouted and jumped about, blew a whistle and banged saucepan lids. He even tried an imitation of old Mrs Cox from school.

"That should really scare him!" said Craig.

To begin with Flow would wheel around to see what was happening, or at least he would try to as Oliver held on hard to his collar and made him keep walking straight ahead. But quite soon Flow began to improve, even though Craig's attempts to distract him got more bizarre and more dramatic. He even begged a huge misshapen garden pot from Dad and smashed it on the stone floor.

"I hope you're going to clear that up, Craig!" shouted Mum's voice from inside the house. But as the distractions got bigger and better, Flow took less and less notice of them. Craig finally got bored with trying to make him circle as he used to, and Oliver was happy that Flow was cured of the problem.

As the summer weeks passed, Mum laughed at

what she called her "gangly pair of boys". Flow's legs grew long and thin. They got him into trouble when he found that his new height allowed him to steal food off the kitchen table, but of course they let him run faster as well. Oliver's legs grew too. His new summer trousers soon flapped above his ankles, but he knew that he, too, was becoming a faster runner.

Elongated dog and boy were both a bit clumsy. Flow's tail grew thick and strong and feathery and with one happy wag of it he could swipe Dad's pots off low shelves or even knock over a small child. Oliver simply bumped into things or tripped over his own feet.

"Who needs an elephant when they've got a brother like that?" Dad asked Sally as Oliver accidentally knocked part of her supper on to the floor. Then, as Flow wolfed down the spilled food, "Still, at least he's got a vacuum-cleaner dog to clear up the mess!"

By the end of August, Flow was more dog than puppy and he and Oliver had learned each other's ways. They were ready for the show. Entry forms were completed and, with Dad's help, Oliver slowly and carefully put Flow's name down for the sheepdog under eighteen months competition and the dogs' obstacle race. He also promised Sally that she could take Flow into the ring for the children's pet competition. The dog and owner's race was a free-for-all on the day. There was no entry form for that.

Oliver took Flow for a run up on the fell the evening before the show. They ran better than ever before. Oliver felt his own breathing, his arms and legs, all working smoothly and efficiently, with Flow as just another part of him running along-side. All the parts were working together to make a fast dog and boy team. Looking down from the fell to the valley below, Oliver could see the sheep pens and the beer tent already assembled ready for tomorrow. He could see the show ring too, and the race field, and he felt confident and happy.

"Great!" Oliver cheered himself and Flow as they trotted home. "Tomorrow you could be champion dog, my Flow!"

-7-

Trust You!

Oliver was up early on show day, even though the show didn't begin until late morning. He took Flow for a steady walk with no running and with lots of command practice, and then home for a light breakfast and a bit more grooming. Sally wanted to add a ribbon to Flow's collar, but Oliver said, "No way." Still, it did make him think how handsome Flow would look with a winning ribbon or two.

Mum, Dad, Sally and Oliver all walked together with Flow up the valley to the show field. Once there, they went their separate ways. Mum and Sally went to the big tent to see how their entries had done. Sally had entered a picture of "My Favourite Place" in the children's painting competition. She won't win with that, thought Oliver, not with a picture of a bit of wall. He knew that behind that wall was Sally's secret den where she went to be alone, but the judges didn't know that. Mum had entered a fruit-cake. Gran was famous for her cakes and she had given Mum the recipe, but the cake didn't really look very good. I'll be the prizewinner in the family today, thought Oliver. That'll make a nice change.

Dad said that he was going to look at the sheep in the pens and to see how neighbouring farmers were doing.

"I might get an idea at last for that competition design too. I'm playing with an idea based on those lovely curves on the rams' horns. The only trouble is that I have a feeling that the horns suit the rams rather better than they would suit cups and plates!" And off he went.

Typical Dad, thought Oliver. Never really switches off from his pottery.

Oliver went to find Craig and to prepare for the first of Flow's competitions – the obstacle race.

"Yes, we'll be there when they announce it on the loudspeakers," Mum had promised. Oliver wanted nobody to miss seeing him and Flow in the ring. Meanwhile, he found Craig and Rex over by the Tysons' sheep trailer. Rex was looking clean and groomed, and he and Flow did their customary greeting of a touch of noses and a tail wag. Craig and Oliver looked at each other a little warily – friends and rivals at the same time today.

"Do you think they'll do it as well in the ring as

they did down in our field?" asked Craig. "It's a bit different with all the people and dogs and that."

"I don't know," said Oliver, a knot gradually tightening in his stomach. He'd been wondering the same thing. Flow was used to trips to the Tysons' farm and into the village, but he did seem a bit nervous and twitchy in the big crowd. If I calm myself down, then perhaps it'll calm him down too, he thought. Just act normal, Oliver! And so he said to Craig, "Want an icecream? I'll buy it if you like, and we've got time."

"Yes. Thanks, Potty. Good idea."

A double-scoop cone each filled the time and, as they licked the last sticky bits off their fingers, the obstacle race was announced. Entering the ring near the beginning of the course, they saw who else was in the race for the first time. It was an odd assortment of both people and dogs. A big fat boy with a tiny dachshund ("That'll never jump high enough!" whispered Craig in Oliver's ear), the lady from the post office with her Old English sheepdog ("Well, that one'll get stuck in the pipe!" whispered Oliver back to Craig), and a number of terriers, border collies and mongrels with a mixture of children and adults. Each contestant was handed a number. The number told them the order in which they would race. The fastest one going round clear would be the winner.

"Does that say six, Craig?" asked Oliver.

"Of course it does, Dumbo! And I'm seven, after you."

Laughing and cheering from the crowd accompanied each turn, and as one, two, three and four each finished the course with clear rounds but very different speeds, Oliver's tummy was tightening again. Then number five turned out to be the dachshund and he really couldn't jump over any of the jumps, but the fat boy wouldn't give up. Again and again they ran to jump and the little dog just stopped still and barked. The crowd was laughing and so was Oliver, and that relaxed him again. It was his turn now and he knew that he could do better than that!

There was a white line on the grass to stand behind for the start and as Oliver waited, one leg bent in front of the other and crouched for a fast start, he concentrated on the four jumps and the tunnel that lay ahead. He was going to do this well. The plastic ribbon flapping on posts round the edge of the ring and the blur of noisy people behind it were out of Oliver's mind altogether.

"Come on, Flow!" he whispered as he waited. "We can do it!"

"Get set – go!" shouted the man with the watch and Oliver leapt into action with Flow at his side. Up over the pile of boxes, then a long jump, of

poles with bracken spread between, cleared beautifully. Brilliant! They were going fast and the crowd was shouting. Then the pipe tunnel.

"Go boy, *go!*" commanded Oliver as they raced up to it, and Flow didn't hesitate. Out the other end and round the bend to the sheep hurdle. Again, no problem. A fast run to the last jump – some beer barrels on their sides and then to the finish line where Craig and Rex stood waiting for their turn. Over the line, and Oliver bent over, panting hard, his hands on his knees but so proud and happy he didn't mind the rasping breath at all. Just let any of them try and beat that! he thought.

"Trust you, Potty!" said Craig.

Oliver looked up, eyes still shining but a bit puzzled.

"Good, weren't we!" he panted.

"You daft dollop!" answered Craig, and then the starter man shouted, "Number seven, get set – go!" and he and Rex were off, pounding round the course.

What was he on about? wondered Oliver, and then he saw Dad signalling from the side of the ring.

"That was really fast, Olly, and Flow was perfect, but why did you do the barrel jump last? That should have been your third jump!"

"Which what?" asked Oliver stupidly and beginning to feel a little sick.

"You did the jumps in the wrong order. You were easily the fastest, but you'll be disqualified for that, I'm afraid. Didn't you hear me shouting?"

Oliver couldn't say anything. Of course he'd heard shouting, but he had thought it was cheering. He didn't want to believe what Dad was telling him, but it was all too believable. As Craig said, trust him.

"Don't look like that, Olly," said Dad. "It's only a bit of fun, and you've the other competitions yet to go. None of them need you to do things in order. You'll be all right in them." He put a hand on Oliver's shoulder. Oliver took a deep breath and tried not to care. Craig and Rex came second in the race. The winner was an older sheepdog, but he was still two seconds slower than Oliver and Flow had been.

Their next competition was the sheepdog under eighteen months category. Dogs and owners walked in a line around the show ring while the two judges looked and whispered to one another. Then each dog and owner in turn were called forward into the centre of the ring where they had to walk and then run up and down in front of the judges. Then the dogs sat to be inspected. Oliver was not surprised to find one judge muttering to the other, "Blind in the right eye," when they looked at Flow. He got a yellow "Highly Commended" ribbon, but then so did all the entrants who didn't come first or second. Rex did come first and won a red ribbon and a smart new collar. Oliver remembered the morning when he had first seen all the puppies at Tommy Thompson's farm and had himself picked out Pony/Rex as the biggest and finest of them. But, "What a fluke!" was what he said to grinning Craig.

Next came the children's pets section, and Sally came racing over to collect Flow and take him into the ring. Flow glanced back at Oliver.

"Go with Sally," ordered Oliver, and off Flow went, walking in line with children and dogs, a few cats and one worm carried in a jamjar. The crowd laughed as children dropped leads and dogs ran, cats miaowed miserably, and the noise of woofing, yapping, shouting and crying made any proper competition impossible. The worm won for originality, but Sally came away with a chocolate bar and was happy.

"How are you getting on, Olly?" asked Mum. "You haven't had any lunch yet, and we've eaten most of the sandwiches. Would you like something from the caterer's van?"

Oliver wasn't feeling hungry. All he could think about now was the one last chance, the dog and owner's race. He was more determined than ever that he was going to win that one. He and Flow were certainly faster than Craig and Rex, but who else would be in it? The race wasn't for another hour, though.

"Go on," said Dad. "If you can't have a winning dog, then at least you can have a hot dog. Here, take a fiver and buy yourself something."

"Thanks."

Oliver munched his hot dog and wandered around the show on his own. He didn't want Craig's company just now. He half-watched the best-dressed huntsmen parading in their scarlet coats, fawn breeches and tight boots, each with a highly groomed and very skinny hound at their heel. He glanced at the sheep and saw that the Tysons had won a couple of rosettes that were tied to the pen. He half-listened to farmers talking about how sheep had been lost to a dog running wild on the fell. He walked past the stalls selling waxed jackets and thick sweaters, candy floss and cheap toys. But his mind was really all on the race. As he thought of how he and Flow had run together, almost as if they had been glued together, last night up on the fell, his confidence began to return.

"Come on!" he muttered, checking his watch and aching to get on with it. At last the loudspeakers shouted out a request that all contestants for the dog and owner's race should gather at the top of the field.

"Here we go, Flow!"

The raggle-taggle assortment of dogs and owners that assembled by the start didn't dent Oliver's confidence. None looked particularly keen or fast. But where was Craig? Oliver looked around and saw him standing behind the tape with the rest of the crowd. Craig saw Oliver at the same moment and shouted across to him, "Flipping Rex has run home!"

"Trust Rex!" said Oliver, getting his own back for Craig's earlier remark. Well, there shouldn't be much competition at all, then. Oliver stood in line at the start with Flow at his side, and they waited.

"To your marks. Get set – go!" and they were off. Oliver felt all the tension of waiting ease as he ran, and he ran fast. He was aware of pounding feet and paws behind him but, he realised happily, he and Flow were well in front. With Flow just touching his left leg and running smoothly alongside, Oliver felt like a winner. This is great, he thought, this is really great.

"Come on, Olly! Come on, Flow!" Mum, Dad and Sally were jumping up and down somewhere to his right. Five metres to go and it was surely all his when a child shrieked somewhere and the ground came up and crashed into Oliver. He lay stunned and winded. Others tripped over him and he stayed there on the ground for a moment or two before it dawned on him that he had not won the race. He had fallen just in front of the finishing tape. Why? And then he worked it out. The child's shriek – Flow must have turned to see what it was and had tripped Oliver up.

"Oh, Flow, *why*?" And Oliver lifted his head to see all the faces in the crowd looking at him, looking at him and laughing. It was like the children at school again – always laughing as Oliver made a fool of himself. And, just as he had done that time at school. Oliver ran. He didn't call Flow, didn't even want Flow, but Flow ran beside him anyway, perfectly now that it was too late.

73

"Stay outside!" shouted Oliver when he reached home, and he slammed the door shut in Flow's face and then ran up to his bedroom and slammed that door shut too.

When Mum, Dad and Sally got home from the show, the kettle was put on for tea and they all sat down around the kitchen table. Flow followed them into the house, his tail tucked between his legs in an apologetic way. He sat with his head resting on Sally's lap and his tail thumping the floor whenever anyone glanced down at him or patted his head. But his ears stayed pressed miserably flat down on his head. It was Oliver's attention and praise that he wanted, and Oliver's chair remained empty.

Mum tried to fetch Oliver down for tea. He heard Mum's call and, although he knew that none of the day's disasters were her fault, that didn't stop him from shouting at her,

"I don't want any tea! Leave me alone!"

He sat in his room with his head in his hands and thought of his dad warning him not to get his hopes up too high. He thought of how he, Oliver, had laughed at the fat boy with the dachshund, just as everyone had later laughed at him. Then he thought of how Flow was a failure too, just like him.

Later Mum tried again, and this time Oliver

took his anger out on the wall instead of on Mum. He thumped the wall hard with his fist then took a deep breath and, nursing his throbbing fist in the other hand, he opened his door and followed his mother sulkily downstairs. His family ignored him for a bit, chatting about Mum's cake that hadn't won.

"I think I'll have to christen that recipe the Titanic cake!" laughed Mum. "Gran promised me that it wouldn't sink, and look at it!" She pointed to the cake's sunken middle. "I hope that you'll all eat it up fast and then I won't have to keep remembering how it looked on the table beside Mrs Postlethwaite's beautiful cake! Come on, Oliver, will you help me out?"

Oliver wasn't hungry. He just played with the cake on his plate, rolling it into hard little pellets between a finger and thumb and then flicking them across the room. Mum saw but didn't tell him off. They were all trying hard to humour him.

"Did you hear about the dog that's been killing sheep?" asked Dad. "Mr Tyson said that he had two ewes killed by it last week."

"Olly," said Sally a bit shyly, "would you like a bit of my chocolate that I won? I got some for my picture as well as with Flow. You can have it if you like," and she pushed a bit of slightly melted squashed chocolate across the table to him.

75

Then Mum put a hand on Oliver's head and ruffled his hair. Oliver scowled under the hand.

"You did your best, and you did very well, you know, Olly. You and Flow both. He's only really a puppy still, remember. You only just missed getting prizes, and there's always another year."

But Oliver suddenly knew that it wasn't the lack of prizes that he minded. It was the loss of his dream. All summer long he had worked for a moment of glory that hadn't arrived, and now what? He felt very empty. Now there was just one more day of freedom, and then back to school for a new school year. He hadn't given school a thought for so long, and now that he did remember, it was so close that the empty feeling was filled instantly with a hot panicky feeling of dread. Dad, as he sometimes did, guessed exactly how Oliver's thoughts were working.

"I think, that you'll find that you've caught up a bit with schoolwork, Olly. You've worked hard with me, and you've learned quite a lot. By the way, I meant to tell you – funny thing – I met your new teacher at the show. Tall, youngish fellow called Patrick Shaw."

But Oliver didn't want to think about school at all.

"I'm off to bed," he said, and closed himself into his room once more.

-8-

Is Anybody There?

Late that night Oliver realised guiltily that he had forgotten to feed Flow. He crept downstairs and found that Mum or someone had done it for him. Flow awoke from exhausted sleep at the sound of Oliver and thumped his tail on the floor, glad to see him. But Oliver was still remembering the humiliation of the show.

"Oh, Flow! One idiot is quite enough. With both of us stupid we don't stand a chance!" Flow cocked his head on one side, not understanding the cross tone of Oliver's voice but wanting to please. Oliver sighed and relented and rubbed Flow's white tummy.

"You did your best, boy." He heard himself echoing what Mum had said to him earlier that evening.

Oliver slept badly and woke the next morning with an urgent feeling that he needed to escape. He must get up on to the fell to have a good think alone before the school term closed in on him. One of the good things about having Flow was that his parents were happier to let him go off walking without them.

Mum and Dad usually had a bit of a lie-in on Sunday mornings, but today when Oliver came downstairs he found Dad already munching toast.

"I've an idea for that design, and guess who inspired it? Flow!"

Oliver looked at what Dad was drawing, and Dad explained.

"You know how Flow backs up and goes round in a circle in that funny way? Well, of course you do! Sorry. Sore point – eh? Well, draw that out and look! You get this pattern. Good, isn't it?" And Oliver had to admit that it was. Dad went on, "I could call it Flow Ware. You off somewhere?" he asked, suddenly registering Oliver's walking boots and backpack.

"Yes, just up on the fell."

"Well, take care, Olly. It looks a bit grey out there. Don't stay out too long." He smiled again.

Flow, eager to please, trotted at Oliver's side and kept glancing up, ready to obey any commands. But Oliver didn't bother with any of that today. He just walked fast, glad of the sullen grey sky and threatening black clouds rolling in from the sea behind him. The gloomy weather meant that he would be on his own on the fells today. Even on the riverside path, Oliver and Flow were alone.

Oliver was absorbed in his own thoughts, hands in pockets and face scowling at the path. He didn't notice the sudden bright flight of a kingfisher over to his right or the penknife that somebody had dropped and lost on the path over to his left. He didn't stop and throw sticks down from the bridge into the pool below, and he didn't call in at the Tysons' farm. He strode on and was glad of the steep zigzag climb up the fell that quickly absorbed some of the angry energy simmering within him.

Stopping to pant and regain his breath near the top, he at last began to notice the world around him. He suddenly realised that a chill wind was blowing from the sea and, as he zipped up his waterproof jacket against the wind, he was surprised to see that grey mist rolling up the valley now hid his home from view. Still, it suited his mood to have home, school and the showground hidden. He felt free. Alone. Except for Flow, of course.

Oliver looked down at Flow and felt a rush of love for his dog. After the show he had wished so strongly that Rex had been his dog instead of Flow. He could have won with Pony. He wondered whether his parents ever felt like that about him when he messed things up. Would they like to swap him for a more successful son? Flow looked up at Oliver, head cocked so that the twinkling bright good eye looked upwards. Oliver caught Flow's head in his hands in a gentle caress of pulled ears.

"I wouldn't really swap you," he said. "But what a pair of duds we are!" He thought of how funny he must have looked when Flow tripped him up and then the other runners had fallen over him.

"We'll just have to lump being laughed at – eh, boy? And now Dad's turning you into pots too, so we're both Potty Pilkingtons!" As good humour returned, Oliver lifted his head up again and saw the thickening grey blanket of mist in the valley and more of it on the ridge just above him. He knew that it was time to go home.

"Come, Flow!" he commanded, and turned to go down the zigzag path. But the path was suddenly crossed by four or five sheep, all with the Tyson farm red mark on their backs, and they were running fast on their twiggy thin legs. Sheep would normally find shelter and stay put in this sort of weather. Why were they up and running? Then some distant noises of growling and a sharp scatter of stones and a human cry reached Oliver's ears. At least that was what it sounded like, but could that really be what he had heard? It was all over in a few seconds.

He stood on the path and listened intently for more sounds, but there was nothing now except the distant scatter of stones as the running sheep ran further away down the fell. Then Flow pushed his nose into Oliver's hand, demanding attention. He whined, ran a little way back up the path, and then looked back at Oliver. The message was clear. He wanted Oliver to follow. He had heard the sounds too, and he wanted to follow them.

"Stay, Flow! Just wait a minute!" Oliver cupped his hands around his mouth and shouted.

"Hello! Hello!"

No answer.

"Is anybody there?"

Still no answer, but Flow quivered with an urgent plea that they go up instead of down the fell.

Oliver looked at his watch, looked at the mist that was really closing in on them now, and looked at Flow, poised and ready to climb.

"All right, Flow. But we've got to take it carefully. Come! I'll put you on your lead. We need to stick together in this."

Oliver clicked the lead on to Flow's collar and pulled up the hood of his jacket. Large drops of rain had started to fall and Oliver wanted very badly to get home to hot Sunday lunch and his family. He didn't feel heroic. He felt frightened. But he also felt that he had no choice. It seemed that somebody was in trouble and there was certainly nobody else around to help. As a Cub, and now as a Scout, Oliver had learnt quite a lot about mountain safety and first aid. Well, the first rule was that you didn't go up into the mountains in bad weather. It was too late for that now.

As they climbed the path on to the ridge, the wind hit Oliver in the face, throwing cold wet rain straight at him. They were walking into cloud, he realised, and visibility was poor. The chilling rain soaked through Oliver's jeans in minutes, making them cling coldly to his legs. He had to work his legs hard to bend them and walk in the wet trousers, but he carried on. Oliver hoped that the strong wind might blow the cloud and rain away, but a rumble of thunder in the distance and the dark thickness of the mist around him gave him little hope that that might happen soon. Flow, unhindered by the rain, led the way. He went confidently but carefully, head always on one side and listening.

"Just keep to the path, Flow, or we'll be in real trouble."

But suddenly Flow was pulling away from the path, wanting to head down from the ridge and on to the steep slope that faced the valley. There was no path here.

"No, Flow! It's too dangerous! Oh, come on, Flow! Let's go home! We probably just heard some animals or something. This is daft!" Oliver was seriously frightened now.

"Flow, *come!*" But Flow wouldn't. Oliver pulled on the lead, but Flow pulled back. He barked and pulled, tugging Oliver down the slope and into a tangle of boulders and bracken and heather and bog. This was the wild steep land where the buzzards nested and it led towards the plunging cliff-drop of a big waterfall. Oliver could hear the roar of water pouring over the fellside to rocks far below, and it wasn't far away. He hesitated, and as he dithered, Flow suddenly pulled hard and Oliver slithered off the path and on to his hands and knees on the slope below. Flow licked Oliver's face and waited while he picked himself up. Soaked, cold and unsure of what he was trying to do, Oliver was in no mood to fight Flow as well as the weather and the mountain.

"You win, Flow. But take it carefully!"

Oliver had never experienced Flow in such a sure and defiant mood before. The slightly cowering, eager-to-please dog of earlier that morning had gone. Now Flow was clearly in charge. Oliver could see little more than grey mist and hear nothing but the waterfall's growing roar. He concentrated hard on placing his feet and not twisting an ankle. He marvelled at Flow's certainty about where he was going. Still, they do say that if you're lost in the dark then you should ask a blind man to help, he thought. All dogs had a good sense of smell, of course, but perhaps Flow's half-blindness and half-deafness had heightened his other senses? He was used to relying on clues other than sight. So, both frightened and a bit excited now, Oliver let Flow guide him further down the steep and slippery slope.

Suddenly Flow stopped, backed up against Oliver's legs, and then went round in a half circle. He peered into the mist with his good eye, and then gave one excited bark and ran so hard that he tugged the lead out of Oliver's hand.

"Flow!" yelled Oliver. He followed, and then almost tripped over a bundle on the ground that

Flow was nosing and whimpering and licking at. But it wasn't just a bundle. It was a boy.

Oh God, please don't be dead, was Oliver's first thought screaming silently in his head. As he crouched down to look at the boy his insides were jumping around and his hands shook. He bent over to see the boy's face.

"Craig!"

Craig was lying, slumped on his side at the bottom of a steep rock outcrop. He looked strangely twisted and he was unconscious.

-9-

What Now?

"Craig!" shouted Oliver again, shaking the boy's shoulder, but there was no response. Oliver bent down and put his cheek to Craig's mouth. He held his breath, and then almost sobbed it out again as he felt the slight warm wind of air coming from his friend's mouth. So he was breathing. What now? he wondered. Don't move him. That might injure him further. But what then? Oliver fought to stir up memories of the first-aid lessons that he'd had. Then he remembered. Check breathing. He'd done that. Good. Now look for injuries. Oliver carefully felt around Craig's head and neck, firmly over the shoulders and then down Craig's body as far as he could feel without moving the unconscious boy. It was when he got to Craig's right leg that he suddenly snatched his hand away and shook it hard as if to shake away the sensation of what he had just felt; two bumps halfway between the knee and the ankle where no bones should end.

"Just get on with it, Potty," he told himself, trying desperately to pull himself together. He rolled up Craig's trouser leg to see with relief that the bone, while clearly making odd lumps in the leg, at least hadn't broken through the skin. There was no blood to cope with.

"OK," he said to Craig, to Flow, to himself, he didn't know. It helped keep control of things somehow to talk aloud. "OK, so now I just keep him warm until help arrives."

Oliver dug into his backpack and pulled out his spare pair of socks and the shiny thin silver survival blanket that he'd always carried but never used before. It didn't look much. Still, he tucked the

blanket over Craig and put the socks over his cold hands.

That won't keep him very warm while he's lying on cold wet rocks, he thought. He was torn between the importance of keeping Craig warm and the importance of not moving him. He unzipped his own jacket and draped that over the boy as well. Then he made Flow lie down, back to back with Craig to share a bit of body warmth. And using Flow made him wonder where Rex was, and how Craig came to be here with a broken leg. He must have fallen down that rock face. In the thick mist Oliver couldn't see how high it was. But that wasn't important. His immediate problem was how to get help fast.

Oliver began to shiver now that he had no jacket on and had stopped walking. The rain soon soaked through the layers of clothes to his skin and the wind blew away his body warmth. I'm probably suffering from shock too, he thought, and knew that he needed help for himself as well as for Craig. After all, he was off the path and visibility was so bad that to try and get down the mountain now would be dangerous. He'd just end up like Craig at the bottom of some other rock face. So what was he going to do? Signal for help, that was it.

As Oliver racked his brains and searched

through his backpack to see if he could find his whistle, Craig stirred and moaned. Flow leapt up and licked at Craig's bruised face, and a hand came up to slap the dog away. He's not paralysed then, thank goodness, thought Oliver as he crouched down again beside his friend. His stomach churned as he looked closely at the ghostly pale bruised face. Would Craig have lost his memory? Sometimes that could happen. What if Craig didn't recognise him?

"Craig, it's me – Oliver. It's Potty!"

Craig's eyes fluttered open and then closed again and he moaned. A moment later his eyes opened and stayed open. He looked at Oliver.

"What . . ." he began, but then he tried to move, to turn and face Oliver, and pain sharp as a knife stab twisted and whitened his face.

"Oh, my leg, my leg!"

Oliver eased Craig's shoulders down to the ground again.

"Don't try to move, Craig. You've broken your leg. But tell me, what happened? Where's Rex?"

"Rex?" Craig was still dazed, but Oliver saw fear sweep any remaining colour from the boy's face as the memory of what had happened flooded back.

"Oh, Rex! Rex ran. He went. He was too scared. He's probably run home. I ran too. But – but it followed me! It wanted me, not Rex. It's teeth! They snapped, and, and, I just ran." Craig was in tears now, waving his battered hands in the air and talking fast. He looked at Oliver and realised that Oliver didn't know what he was talking about. He made a big effort to pull himself together and began his story again, still shakily, but more slowly and steadily than before.

"You see, I wanted to see this dog they've all been talking about. The one that's been killing sheep. My dad and some of the others, they were talking about getting up a team to hunt it down, and I thought I'd take Rex with me and see if I could find it. I didn't want to catch it or anything, not on my own. I'm not stupid. I just wanted to see what it looked like. Anyway, I got up on the fell and saw all these sheep running. Loads of them, all running fast and not caring where they ran. Some of them were getting hurt. They were in a real panic. They were from our farm and they were running from that dog! It was coming after them much faster than they could run. It grabbed one of the sheep and rolled it on the ground. It was like those films on telly where a lion catches a gazelle – you know. Anyway, it had its teeth round this sheep's throat and the sheep sort of screamed. It was horrible! I hated that dog for doing that to our sheep, and I picked up some stones and threw them at it and shouted. Then it just dropped the sheep and turned on me."

Craig wiped tears and rain away from his eyes, and then went on. "When it got to me it jumped on its back legs and it was so big and strong and its mouth black and slobbery with big teeth that were snapping in my face. It was trying to knock me over so that it could get me on the ground, just like the sheep! It wanted to kill me! It was too strong for me to fight, so I just ran. I only ran a few steps and then I tripped and fell down. But not just down to the ground, Potty. Down and down and . . ." Craig suddenly turned to one side and was sick. He started to shake all over.

Oliver took his backpack and tipped out all that was left in it. He gently eased Craig's head and shoulders up and then down on to the empty bag as a sort of pillow.

"It wanted to kill me, Potty! It really was going to kill me! Oh!" Craig winced with pain as he tried again to move into a more comfortable position.

"How bad is my leg?"

"It's broken below your knee. I'll put some padding around it, but then we've just got to wait for help. I was going to whistle for help when you woke up."

But Craig wasn't listening. Oliver saw the dreadful thought come into his mind.

"Is the dog still here, Potty? Where is it?" Craig's terrified eyes were suddenly darting, searching around for a sign of the dog.

"I've not seen or heard it since I heard you fall," said Oliver, but the thought made his stomach churn too.

"Flow would know if there was another dog about."

"Yes," said Craig. Then, after a pause, "Rex just went home, you know. He just left me."

"That might be the best thing, though," said Oliver. "Your mum and dad will call out the rescue when he gets home without you."

"But they aren't at home! There's nobody at home today, not until tea-time. They've gone off for my new cousin's christening. I didn't want to go." Craig was shaking and crying. Oliver, soaked and cold and finding the comforting thought of help on its way now gone, tried to keep calm. Craig couldn't be expected to do anything. He would have to think for both of them.

"Well, don't worry, mate. I'll try whistling and see if anyone answers. We aren't far above the valley. Someone must hear."

Oliver found the whistle from his backpack and put it to his lips. What was the proper signal? His mind went blank again and he could feel panic knocking at the door of his stomach and wanting to come in. He closed his eyes tight and pushed the panic away as he remembered. Six blasts on the whistle, then wait a minute and then do it again. He looked gratefully at the timer watch that Mum had given him, and he pushed buttons to set it to bleep every minute. Then he blew six shrill blasts. He and Craig strained their ears through the next minute as they waited for a reply.

"What are they supposed to do to let us know they've heard us?" asked Craig.

"It should be three long whistles, but then somebody might hear us who hasn't got a whistle on them to reply with. If your dad were upon the fell with his sheep, would he have a whistle?"

"No, but he could stick his fingers in his mouth and do it. Or shout!"

For sixteen eternal minutes Oliver whistled and then both boys waited eight times over. Around them all was silent except for the ever-present rumble of the waterfall. Then a sudden flurry of hail, hard, cold and stinging, swept over them. They were getting colder with every passing minute.

"This is stupid!" said Oliver. "There's nobody around. There's not much point in whistling at nothing for ever. Let's leave it for a bit and then try again. I'm frozen."

Oliver got up and shook and brushed the frozen lumps of hail from his hair and clothes. He wrapped his arms around himself in an effort to keep warm. It didn't help much, and he looked down at Craig.

"How are you doing?" he asked Craig. He didn't really need Craig to reply. The pale shivering face, screwed up with pain, told him that Craig needed help as soon as possible.

"Tell you what!" he said as brightly as he could. "I'll make a shelter over you to keep the weather off you!" That sounded good, but he wasn't sure how he was going to do it. Oliver set to work collecting some old fence posts tangled in a mess of rusty barbed wire, some sticks and some biggish stones. Then he wondered what to do with them. He realised that the activity was warming him up nicely, but wouldn't do much to help Craig. Not until it was finished. Craig needed something to warm him now. Oliver delved into his pocket and found a few boiled sweets that he had put there some days ago. The wrappers were sticky and covered with pocket fluff, but inside the sweets looked OK.

"Here you are, Craig. Suck this, and there's a few more when you've finished that one."

Why had he so stupidly eaten his emergency food and not replaced it? Oliver remembered the evening before the show when he and Flow had felt like champions up on the fell. He had broken open the emergency chocolate bar and shared it with Flow. Annoyance with his own stupidity gave Oliver angry strength. He pulled at the coarse, sharp bracken stems and piled up the feathery fronds ready for his shelter while he tried to think. Craig was lying across the slope of the fell and the wet rainy wind was blustering up the valley from his head end. The main thing, Oliver decided, was to give shelter from that wind. "Wind Chill Factor" kept repeating itself in his mind. Both he and Craig were soaked already, so there was little to be gained by roofing out the rain. But that wind could whip away what body heat they still had and make them even more dangerously cold. Besides, if he tried building a roof, Oliver felt sure that he would drop things on to Craig. So, stopping every so often to blow six more blasts on the whistle, Oliver made a criss-cross of sticks and fence posts behind Craig's head.

"What are you doing, Potty?" asked Craig through chattering teeth.

Flow got up as if to help.

"Flow, stay!" ordered Oliver. He was determined that if Craig couldn't have proper food to warm him, then at least the dog could be a hot-water bottle. And then he told Craig what he was doing and he kept on chattering of this and that, rather as he had once chatted soothingly to tiny Flow when the puppy had been frightened of the thunderstorm.

Digging into the fell would be difficult. He had no spade and the fell was mostly made up of stones anyway, so instead of digging in the ends of his sticks, he piled stones around them to hold them in place. Then he drew out the string from the waist of his jacket and joined it to the string from the neck of his backpack and used them to bind the posts together where they crossed. After that, he simply piled up bracken behind the crossed posts to form a windbreak. He carefully made sure that all the stems pointed upward and the fronds downward in order to throw the rain off and away. The stones and the sharp bracken stems cut and bruised Oliver's hands as he worked, but his hands were so numbed by cold and wet that he hardly felt them and he went on working as fast as he could. It was important to shelter Craig, but it also helped Oliver to be busy. He was rather pleased with the windbreak.

"It keeps my head and neck a bit warmer anyway," said Craig encouragingly, but it didn't stop Craig's violent shivering and that worried Oliver a lot. He knew that you were more likely to die on a mountain from exposure than from a broken leg.

"Don't worry. I'll do one at the other end too, and then build it up along your side that isn't sheltered by the mountain. Then the wind will really be off you. I'll just try whistling again first, though.

If only help would come! As he whistled, Oliver looked at his watch. Still only twelve o'clock. It felt as if they had been up here for hours and hours and yet it was only just an hour since he had found Craig. Would Mum and Dad be missing him yet? For once Oliver very much hoped that they *would* be fussing. He tried to send a telepathic message to tell them to call out the mountain rescue. Six more shrill blasts of the whistle and then once again he and Craig listened to the quiet around them. Against the background rumble of the waterfall, all was silent. Even the birds seemed to keep quiet in this wet mist, and the sheep had all run away when the dog had attacked.

Then Flow suddenly growled low in his throat He jumped up from his place beside Craig, and the hairs, on his back rose up. He growled again more loudly. Oliver felt the hair on his own head seem to rise up too as a distant noise of something moving on loose stones came to him. Craig's eyes had become great circles of fear. He had heard it too. Oliver crouched down close beside him. Boys and dog waited. Silence. And then the scrunch of something coming slowly and surely nearer.

Suddenly Craig laughed out loud. He raised

himself up a bit, propped up on his elbows. He grabbed Oliver's sleeve.

"Potty, it's only the m –" But Oliver clamped a hand over Craig's mouth and lifted a finger quickly to his own mouth to tell Craig to keep quiet. Flow crouched down into a position ready to spring into action. It was the same position that he got into when he was waiting for Oliver to throw a stick, but this time his lips curled back, his teeth showing white and pointed, and the growl rumbled softly in his throat. The growl was more vibration than noise. All Oliver could really hear was still just the threatening rumble of the waterfall through which the intermittent sounds of movement came. Sometimes the scrunching noises disappeared as whatever it was stepped on soft grass, but then sounded again on the loose scree.

"But . . ." Again Oliver's hand silenced Craig. He knew that Craig was thinking the noise might be rescuers at last, but Oliver was certain that whatever was coming towards them was something much less friendly than that. Rescuers wouldn't pant. He bent down and hissed into Craig's ear, "Rescuers would be calling our names. It isn't them!"

Craig's eyes grew suddenly wider still and his breathing fast and shallow. Oliver knew what was coming towards them through the mist, and he could see from Craig's face that he did too.

Oliver moved the jacket up from around Craig's chest and legs so that it covered the boy's head. Craig was covered from head to toe by survival blanket and jacket. Would that protect him? Oliver wondered about himself next. His eyes darted around, searching quickly for some sort of weapon. Something to hold in his hand. He picked up the biggest of the fence posts that he could reach without having to move from his guard of Craig, and then he waited. He and Flow stood ready for the longest twenty seconds of Oliver's life, and then suddenly the waiting and the quiet ended.

-10-

No!

Out of the mist, the huge black mass of the killer dog sprang straight at Oliver. Craig screamed from under the jacket. But as the dog sprang, so did Flow. Flow was far too small against the big dog's muscle-bound bulk to stop the leap, but he pushed the dog to land to one side of Oliver. The silence that had held for so long was gone as the two dogs hurled themselves at each other in a snarling, fierce fight.

Oliver, hands grasping the stick and breath shallowly panting, watched as the huge dog leapt on Flow. Flow looked very small and slight beside the massive bulk of the big dog. But, snarling and lunging, Flow was like a wild dog himself as he snapped with his long wolf-like fangs. He sank his teeth into the great meaty shoulder of the big dog. The big dog tossed about wildly, trying to throw Flow off. But Flow, lifted off his feet and whipped to and fro, hung on. As the big dog swung Flow

crashing into the rock face, Oliver saw bright fresh blood spurt from Flow's head as he hit the jagged stone. Suddenly Oliver was more angry than frightened. He gave a great shout of fury.

"No!"

Then he raised the fence post above his head. Taking two leaping steps forward, he brought the stick crashing down on the dog's nose. Oliver shouted again and raised the stick. This time the dog reared up to meet the blow and to try and snatch the stick from his grasp, but Oliver brought it whacking down in a sideways blow to one of the dog's front legs. The dog yelped in pain and crumpled to the ground.

Oliver raised the stick again, this time clasping both ends in his next attack, but as he did so, the dog turned and began to limp away. Its face cowered and growling, head held down and glancing defensively back at Oliver, the dog hopped on three legs in an ungainly hurry away into the mist. The uneven scrunch of its hobbling got more distant and gradually faded to nothing. But still Oliver stood with the stick clenched in front of his chest and his muscles sprung tight for action.

"God, Potty! You beat him!" Oliver turned to see a white-faced Craig peeping out from under the jacket. Oliver sobbed out a breath, let his arms come down and dropped the wooden post to the ground. He began to shake all over.

"Flow!" he said, stooping and picking up the injured dog into his arms. Sticky blood covered Flow's head and dripped down on to Oliver's sleeves. But the little dog looked brightly at Oliver with his one good eye, as if to say, "I'm all right!" and Oliver felt Flow's tail thump a wag. Suddenly Oliver sat down. His legs seemed to have turned to mush and wouldn't hold him up any longer. He sat, shivering, clutching Flow, and unable to do anything else for some time. His muddled brain told him in a far-off way that he should be bandaging the wound on Flow's head, should be whistling again for help, should be seeing if Craig was all right, but his body wouldn't move. Craig propped himself painfully up and now it was his turn to try and talk Oliver out of the shock that was paralysing him. He talked, and gradually Oliver's brain began to register what was being said.

"Hey, Potty, what's black and white and red all over? Flow!" and then, as Craig saw from Oliver's face that this time he had been heard, "Oh, sorry. That's not really funny. But I think you ought to do something about Flow's head. I'll hold him for you if you like."

Oliver was brought back to his senses, and suddenly realised that Flow was losing a lot of blood. He got to his feet in a wobbly way and put Flow down beside Craig.

"What can I use?" he asked Craig. He needed to be told what to do. His brain was as mushy as his legs.

"If you can reach into my trouser pocket you'll find a clean hankie. My mum always puts one there." And Craig lifted the silver blanket and clenched his teeth tight as Oliver pulled the handkerchief out. Oliver folded it into a pad and held it gently and firmly down on the wound just above Flow's right ear. Craig was still giving the orders.

"I can hold that on Flow's head. He's not going to move. And you can try whistling again."

Oliver just wished that somebody would come and take over, wrap them up warmly and take all three of them home. He didn't think he could take much more. He numbly raised the whistle to his lips and blew six blasts that told anyone listening that they needed help, urgently.

The bleeding on Flow's head slowed and he seemed happy to rest beside Craig with the pad held gently to his wound. Suddenly Oliver knew that *he* wanted to lie down and rest too. He was too tired, too wet and too shivering with cold to do more. Anyway, wasn't it good mountain-rescue technique for people to huddle together to share body heat?

"Hey, lift up the blanket, Craig. I'm going to lie down with you for a bit." Oliver began to move round to Craig's side.

"No, you're not!" said Craig.

"Why not? It's a good idea! It'll help keep you

warm and, anyway, I want a sleep!" Oliver was furious. He had been the one doing all the work. He had made the shelter. He had fought the dog. And now he wanted a rest. What was wrong with that?

"Why not?" he asked again, angrily.

"Because it's a stupid idea, that's why!" answered Craig. "If you lie down now you'll go to sleep.We'll both go to sleep and we'll never wake up again. That way we'll *die*, Olly!"

"Well, what do *you* suggest, then?" Oliver ached to lie down and close his eyes, and anyway, he couldn't think of anything else he could do.

"You've got to go for help, Potty! You've got to!" Then, as Oliver didn't reply, "Look, it's not that far. And . . ." Craig paused. "And I don't think I can keep going much longer. I keep seeing black dots swimming around."

That shook Oliver's numbed brain and he looked at Craig. His face was paper white and the whole of his body shook. He knew that Craig was right. He would have to go.

"OK, then. I'll go."

Now, he thought, he must do this properly or things could be made even worse. He glanced through the bits and pieces that had come out of his backpack and were now scattered on the ground. He selected the compass and left the rest.

Craig's shivering worried Oliver badly. In a panic of wanting to do something for his friend, he hurriedly put all the bits of bracken that he had pulled but not yet used over Craig's body. Perhaps that would keep him a bit warmer. But then he thought that it might camouflage Craig too much. It covered up the bright yellow of the jacket and the silver of the blanket. Perhaps rescuers wouldn't see him under it? And he pulled all the bracken off again.

"God, Potty, just *go!*" stuttered Craig through chattering teeth.

"OK. Sorry. Look, I'll leave Flow with you and I'll write a note and leave that with you too, just in case you pass out or something."

Oliver found a slightly damp piece of paper and a stub of pencil and tried to remember what should be put into a rescue note. Time and place and names and injuries? Something like that. Hating more than ever his slowness at writing, he concentrated as hard as his stupid-feeling mind would let him, and he wrote:

Oliver tucked the note behind the jacket on Craig's chest so that it wouldn't get any wetter.

"Right, then, shall I bring you fish and chips, or a beefburger?" He tried to joke. He was frightened of saying goodbye.

"Oh, bring us a Coke, please," said Craig. "I'm dying for a drink!" Oliver didn't laugh, though. That was too close to the truth to be funny. Instead he set his compass to point northwards, down towards the valley bottom.

"I've put the whistle by your side, Craig. Leave it a bit to give me time to get help, and then blow it to help the rescuers find you. Here, you can have my watch too. Then you'll know how the time is going." He paused. "You can keep it if you like. Afterwards. I mean." Then Oliver turned to Flow before Craig could say anything.

"Flow, stay!" Oliver held his hand, flat palm in front of Flow's face to show that he really meant it. Flow whined and stirred uneasily, but he stayed as he was told to at Craig's side.

"See you soon," said Oliver, and he stepped down and away. Moments later, as the mist enveloped him, Flow was there again at Oliver's side, a sheepish look on his face.

"Oh, Flow! Poor Craig! Still, it's nice to have you with me. You've probably got more sense of where to go than I have, anyway." And as he carefully made his way down the steep slope, Oliver was very glad to have Flow beside him.

-11-

The Two of Them Together

However much he tried to concentrate, Oliver knew that his brain was numbed and his thoughts drifted. He hurried, eyes aching as he strained to see through the mist and rain. As he climbed and stumbled over the rough steep ground, he was searching all the time for a real path that would guide him down safely. He trusted Flow's instincts and let him lead the way. He thought of home and food and warmth and rest, and then he thought of wounded Craig, quite alone on the mountainside. Then he thought of the big dog. Could it possibly come back and attack again? Just as that thought tightened his stomach, Oliver heard a noise. What was it? Not the big dog again, oh please! He clenched his frozen fists in a wishing prayer. He just hadn't the strength left to cope with that! But then he listened and knew that the noise wasn't anything to do with the dog this time. It was a man's voice, shouting. Oliver listened hard, his heart pounding in excitement, and he could just make out some of the words.

"Oliv . . . Olive . . . *Oliver*!"

The man was shouting his name!

"Over here!" he tried to shout back, but it came out as a croak. He tried again.

"Help! Over here!"

The other voice gradually came nearer.

"We've found you, lad. Great! I'm almost with you. Just stay where you are and keep calling!"

"I'm here. I'm here!" Oliver shouted in an increasingly shaky voice and he braced himself, feet apart, to stop himself from falling over. He felt as if the last drop of energy had left his body. And as the man emerged out of the mist Oliver sat down suddenly and cried big wet tears that couldn't be stopped. He felt vaguely surprised that the tears came out so hot when he felt as if every bit of him was so cold. Then the tall figure of the man crouched beside him and put an arm around Oliver's shoulder.

"Hey there," he soothed. "You're all right now. You've been found. I'll just call the other rescuers and tell them where we are, and then we'll sort you out a bit."

The man pulled out a walkie-talkie and spoke into it.

"Eric? Patrick here. I've found the boy. Yes. Yes.

I think he's just shaken, and very wet and cold of course, but I'll call you back when I've talked to him. Give his parents the good news! Yes. Great. Yes, we're about two hundred metres east of the waterfall, at about the same height as the spot where we parted. Yes, and I don't think you'll need to call out the stretcher party." Then, "Oh, hang on, will you, Eric?" Oliver was shaking the man's arm.

"Up there!" he sobbed, fighting to speak through the tears and shaking that still wouldn't stop.

"What's this?" asked the man, gently encouraging Oliver. "You've a friend who's hurt up there?" Oliver nodded dumbly.

"OK. We'll get help to him in no time, don't you worry." And then he was talking to Eric again on the walkie-talkie. When he finished he took his rucksack off his back and began to pull out jumpers and jackets and gloves and a Thermos flask.

"Right now, Oliver. Eric and a couple of others will be here in a minute or two. Then we'll find your friend and get you both off this mountain and home before you know it. Now, while we wait, let's sort you out a bit." As he talked, the tall rescue man was gently easing Oliver into warm layers of clothing and Oliver limply let him do it all, feeling too much like a ragdoll to even lift his own arms into armholes. A plastic cup of sweet hot chocolate was placed in his shaking hands. Oliver thankfully sipped and only half-listened to the man's words that seemed to float around his head but never quite enter his brain. A bar of chocolate followed the drink. As his tummy warmed, his mind seemed to warm and begin to work again too.

"Are you coming round a bit now, Oliver?" The man could see the difference in him. He began to talk business, still gently, but looking Oliver in the eye and holding his attention.

"Now then. Your friend, Craig. You say he has a broken leg? Can you tell me exactly what happened?"

Haltingly at first, but then in more and more of a rush, Oliver told him about finding Craig, about the broken leg, about the dog. By the time he had finished, three other rescuers had arrived and waited, listening, until Oliver had finished. Then the leader, Eric, took charge.

"Can you lead us back up to Craig?" he asked Oliver, and Oliver nodded his head. The warmth and food and drink and, even more than that, the fact that help was now here, had renewed his strength a bit and he wanted to get those same comforts to Craig.

"He's up this way," Oliver said. He got to his

feet, helped by the tall rescue man. Patrick put a strong hand under Oliver's elbow to lift him. As Oliver stepped once again up the fell, he was glad to have Flow who, with comforting certainty, led the way. Eric blew his whistle and shouted and they all heard the excited repeated whistling in reply from somewhere up the slope. Oliver smiled with relief.

"That's him!" he said.

"Fine. We can find him now," said Eric. "Patrick can take you down the mountain if you like, Oliver, and we'll see to Craig." But Oliver wanted to go on now.

"OK, lad. But you take it gently with Patrick and we'll go on ahead."

Eric and the two others set off fast up into the mist and rain and soon disappeared from sight. Their voices shouted in the distance as they hurried help to Craig.

Oliver smiled. Craig was being rescued at last.

"My dog knew the way," he told Patrick, "even in the mist. He's much better at it than I am."

"Yes," said Patrick, his arm still supportingly round Oliver's shoulder as they paced slowly upwards. "It was your dad who raised the alarm when you didn't get home in time for lunch, and he mentioned the dog. A fine little dog, he told me. But we didn't know about Craig. It was lucky for him that you were up on the fell. Otherwise he might not have had the rescue looking for him for some hours yet by the sound of it."

They walked on in silence for a bit, and then Patrick said, "By the way, as from tomorrow I believe that I'm to be your teacher! My name is Patrick Shaw – Mr Shaw to you at school, I suppose, but plain Patrick up here on the fell."

"Oh." Oliver didn't know what else to say. What a change this Mr Shaw would be from old Mrs Cox! But the thought of his finding out how bad Oliver was at schoolwork was embarrassing.

As they neared the voices and lights that marked the place where Craig and the rescuers were, Flow ran back and forth between Craig and Oliver, pleased with himself for bringing them together again and yapping in his old high-pitched puppy way. Oliver picked him up. Flow licked Oliver's face and Oliver hugged him back. He wondered how much of the tensions and dramas of the last couple of hours Flow had felt. He seemed so happy and lighthearted now.

"Oh, Flow!" he laughed. "You're the best!"

When they reached the rescue party, the men were busy with first aid and a hot drink and blankets, while Eric summoned a stretcher party to carry Craig down the mountain.

"There's a party with a stretcher being gathered

now," he said, and then, as he spotted Oliver, "your dad is one of them. They'll need a dozen or more strong volunteers before they can set off." Oliver looked surprised and Eric laughed. "They don't all carry it at once, you know! On steep rough ground like this, they'll be passing the stretcher from hand to hand. It's hard work and the more people who share it the better. And there'll be a helicopter

ready to meet the stretcher in the field at the bottom of the fell."

Craig's pale face grinned at Oliver from within the folds of a red blanket. He looked like a funny old lady in a shawl. Or, thought Oliver, like a newborn baby. He remembered the wizened look of tiny blanket-wrapped baby Sally when he had held her in his arms soon after she was born.

"Did you hear that, Potty? A helicopter! In our field!"

Oliver smiled back. If Craig was well enough to enjoy the excitement of the rescue, then there couldn't be too much wrong with him.

"Now then," said Patrick, "what about this little dog of yours?" And, Oliver realised that he had been dumbly clutching Flow for his own comfort, without giving a thought to Flow's wound. Patrick gently took Flow and sat down to make a lap for the dog to lie on. He probed the sticky matted mess of blood and hair on Flow's head.

"Not bad at all," he said. "Head wounds always bleed a lot. It'll probably need a stitch or two, but I don't think the bone has been broken. What do you call him?" he asked Oliver.

"Flow."

"Nice name. Nice dog," he said as he gently stroked Flow's coat and Flow wagged an appreciative reply.

"Now you just sit here with young Flow, and I'll gather all your bits and pieces together. Then shall you and I start back for home? There'll be a bit of a wait for the stretcher party. And once they get Craig sorted and strapped on to the stretcher, they'll be off down the fellside fast. If we go now, they'll probably catch up with us. What do you say?"

"Yes," said Oliver. Sitting down, he was going cold and numb again and he wanted more than anything to get home and to get Flow to a vet. He soothed and stroked his dog as Patrick began to gather the scattered possessions into Oliver's backpack. Oliver watched and saw the man pause, pick something up, and look at it for a moment. It was the rescue note that he had left with Craig.

"Did you write this, Oliver?" he asked. Oliver nodded miserably and his ears went pink with embarrassment. It was sure to be full of mistakes. His writing always was. This Mr Shaw was a teacher – was he about to say, "And how old are you, Oliver Pilkington? Are you four years old or ten?" in that sarcastic voice that Mrs Cox used?

"Hey, you're dyslexic, aren't you?" was what he actually said.

"What?" said Oliver in surprise.

"This writing. It looks to me as though you're dyslexic. Like me, as a matter of fact! Do you have trouble with reading and writing? With number work? Perhaps with telling right from left, up from down, that sort of thing?"

"Yes," said Oliver, "but Mrs Cox calls it being backward, not dis – whatever you said."

"Oh yes. I know. They called me backward, too. But you're certainly not that. Just look at the way you handled things today!" Then, as he saw Oliver's ears going tell-tale pink again, this time in happy embarrassment, "Come on, lad. We're all sorted and Flow seems steady on his feet. Let's set off, and I'll tell you about dyslexia as we go, if you like."

Oliver went over to where Craig was being propped up and given some pain-killing pills. He wasn't sure what to say.

"See ya, Craig. I'll get Mum to bring me to see you in hospital."

"Yeah. 'Bye."

They grinned at one another.

Patrick, Oliver and Flow went slowly and carefully down the fellside. The mist was lifting a bit, but it still hid the valley and the mountain-tops. It felt private. They talked about dyslexia. Patrick had some funny stories to tell of silly situations he had got into as well as the frustrations that his own dyslexia had caused. That was before he learnt to overcome most of the problems it brought. Oliver told him what had happened at the show in the obstacle race, and then they talked about dogs. Patrick said that the wild dog would be caught and put down. It would be done without its feeling any pain. And Patrick said that he had had a sheepdog when he was a boy in Ireland. She had been called Hannah. Then Oliver suddenly stopped walking.

"Mr Shaw."

"Yes."

"You know I said my dog is called Flow?"

"Yes."

"Well, actually that's only his name backwards. Written backwards, I mean. They said that he was backward too, you see. His real name is Wolf!"

Patrick looked puzzled for a moment, and then he laughed.

"Hey, that's great! And it sounds as though he lived up to his real name today!" Then he chuckled. "You know, that fits my old dog too, when you think about it. She was as steady and straight as they come, and Hannah written backwards spells . . . Hannah!"

"Nobody else knows that's his real name yet," Oliver went on. "It was a sort of secret. It seemed such a big name for a little puppy, especially a puppy with only one good eye and ear."

"Well, I think it's about time you told everyone, don't you?" replied Patrick. "He's proved himself today. He's a faithful friend and a fighter, and I think Wolf suits him very well."

"I think I'll still call him Flow for everyday, though," said Oliver.

"Well, if you want to, you can tell your dad about Wolf right now!" said Patrick. He nodded downhill to where the stretcher party were emerging from the mist as they walked fast up towards Craig.

"Dad!" Oliver shouted as he spotted his father's distinctive beard and red jacket amongst the group.

"Olly!" And Dad ran the distance between them and hugged Oliver hard against his stiff jacket. "You're so wet!" he laughed. Then, "But are you hurt?" Dad looked intently at Oliver, and Oliver shook his head and smiled to reassure him. "Right then, home you go to your mum and Sally. And look after Flow, too. I gather from the walkie-talkie conversation that he has been the hero in this adventure!"

"Well now," said Patrick. "I think really that honour should go to Oliver here. Or at least to the two of them together."

"Yes," Dad agreed. "You're right. They do belong together, those two." He crouched down to stroke Flow and to look more closely at his wound. Flow licked his hand and Dad held Flow under the chin. "You're an important member of the family now, aren't you, Flow?" Then Dad looked up at Oliver's

119

smiling face. "You were quite right to get him, Olly, quite right." Then, laughing, he straightened up. "Perhaps I should have let Sally have her elephant too, eh? It could've carried the stretcher! Now, I had better go if I'm to be of any help to young Craig. I'll see you both later." Dad shook Mr Shaw's hand, paused for amoment, and then shook Oliver's hand too before turning back up the fell.

At the bottom of the fell a mountain rescue helicopter was waiting in one of the Tyson farm fields and beside it were two Land-Rovers and a group of people. As Oliver stumbled down the last stretch of rock and shale on to the soft field grass, he saw Sally run from the group. She ran straight across the field and hurled herself at him. In his wobbly state, Oliver was almost knocked over by her fierce hug of welcome. And then Mum was there too with a warm strong hug that lifted him off his feet.

Sally was jabbering about helicopters and Flow and blood and police, but, after a kiss and a second hug, all Mum said was, "Hot bath!"

-12-

Not Completely Potty

Oliver went to see Craig in hospital. Craig was sitting up in a big white bed with his plastered leg suspended by a pulley.

They didn't talk about what had happened on the fell. It was all too recent and vivid and they both

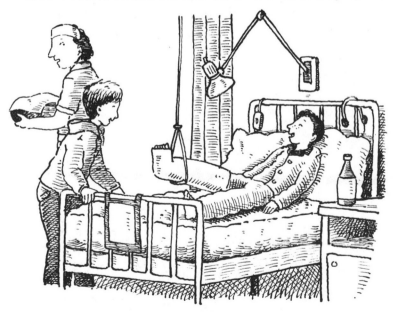

knew how the other felt without putting it into words. But Oliver told Craig about Flow really being called Wolf.

"Tell you what," said Craig. "You can have that collar that Rex and I won at the show if you like. I think that Flow – Wolf, I mean – is a great dog. Great name, too. And you're not completely potty either!" He ducked as Oliver pretended to punch him on the head. "I'll have to call you something different now. How about Peter?"

"Peter!" exclaimed Oliver in surprise. "Why Peter?"

"*Peter and the Wolf*, of course – you wally!" And this time Oliver did thump him.

"Really, boys! This is a hospital, not a playground!" said a starchy nurse as she passed them, and they laughed together.

About the Author

Pippa Goodhart worked as a teacher, a publisher's reader and ran a bookshop before becoming a writer. Over the years Pippa has published more than forty books, ranging from volumes for young readers to longer novels. Pippa still works with children in schools and also teaches adults to write for children. She lives in Leicester with her husband and children.

OTHER BOOKS BY BARN OWL
YOU MIGHT ENJOY

You're thinking about doughnuts
MICHAEL ROSEN
£4.99 ISBN 1-903015-03-0

It was cold, spooky and very boring.

Frank hated Friday nights, sitting in the
museum while his mum did the cleaning.
He felt very alone . . . until a skeleton
came over for a chat.

'How about a doughnut?' asked the skeleton.
'OK.' said Frank.

And suddenly the museum didn't seem quite
so boring any more.

But after a few chilling encounters with some of
the skeleton's weird and wonderful friends
all Frank really wants is his mum . . .

The Dragon Charmer

DOUGLAS HILL

£4.99 ISBN 1-903015-36-7

Elynne is the daughter of a dragon charmer and desperately wants to help her father in his work, but she is a shy girl, easily frightened and the ferocious creatures terrify her. However, when a rare royal dragon – a Crimson Queen – flies into Elynne's life and gives birth to a male baby dragon, there seems to be some kind of strange connection between the baby prince and the girl. When it becomes clear that the baby dragon is in mortal danger, Elynne wonders if she will find the courage to protect him.

A marvellous fantasy from a master of the genre.

Your guess is as good as mine

BERNARD ASHLEY

£3.99 ISBN 1-903015-04-9

The rain hit Nicky hard as he came out of school and everyone ran. It was screams and running feet all along the street, especially when the thunder started. So it seemed too good to be true when he saw his dad's yellow Mini. But it wasn't his dad's car, nor was it his dad driving and Nicky is suddenly plunged into a terrifying adventure and a frantic race against time.